A DEATH AT THE CHURCH

A EUPHEMIA MARTINS MYSTERY

Caroline Dunford

Published by Accent Press Ltd 2019

ISBN 9781786156693
eISBN 9781786156709

Accent Press Ltd
Octavo House
West Bute Street
Cardiff
CF10 5LJ

Chapter One

'Euphemia!' roared Bertram. 'What have you done?'

His eyes focused on the blood spreading across the front of my wedding dress. My legs felt shaky, but I rose from my kneeling position and turned to face him. I reached out to him. My hands were scarlet with blood. Along with Hans, Richenda, and Merry, he was huddled at the small church door leading to the ante-chamber.

'I realise I do not appear to my best advantage, Bertram,' I said. I was proud my voice held. 'But I only did what I had to do.' I shook my head sadly.

Lying on the ground at my feet, Richard Stapleford, my long-held nemesis, gazed up at me with glassy eyes. For once he had nothing cutting to say. In fact, I was almost certain he would never speak again.

The others too seemed frozen in place. It was Hans who moved first. He walked quickly up to me and took me gently by the shoulders. His grey eyes stared unflinchingly into mine. 'Where is the knife?' he said.

'I put it on the ground over there,' I said, indicating a space behind me. 'I do not think it should be kept.' He went to retrieve it. 'Please do not,' I said. 'You will spoil your gloves.'

'I'll keep the others away for as long as I can,' said Richenda. 'It won't be that long. Hurry!' She pushed Merry and Bertram into the room, closing the oak door behind her. Merry stumbled on the step down. Bertram automatically caught her arm, but his eyes had not left my face. He was ashen pale. Even his lips had all but lost their colour.

'Are you alright, Bertram?' I said. 'You look unwell. I know he was your brother, but you cannot say there was any love lost between you.'

Merry gave a little gulping sob. 'Oh, Euphemia!'

'How do you want to handle this, Stapleford,' said Hans from behind me. 'Shall we call it self-defence?'

'Did he attack you?' said Merry, with what I felt was unbecoming eagerness.

'No,' I said. 'Not today. Although he has done in the past.'

'Good God,' said Bertram. 'I didn't know.'

'It was the usual master-preying-on-servant thing,' I said, brushing it aside. 'You must have known he was one of those men who thought nothing of forcing himself on women under his control.'

'I know what he was, Euphemia,' said Bertram. 'But this?'

'I do not believe we can move the body,' said Hans, 'without it being obvious. There is too much blood.'

'Like in Shakespeare,' I said. My vision swam. I took several deep breaths. '*Macbeth.*'

I heard running footsteps. Bertram shook off his dazed state. 'That's it, Euphemia. You must say he attacked you.'

'But he did not,' I said. 'I will not lie. Not here. Not today.' I ran my hands over my ruined dress. 'Do you think Richenda will have something I can borrow?'

Hans came up beside me and studied my face. 'She is in shock, Bertram. She has no idea what she is saying.'

'Faint,' said Bertram desperately.

'But you hate it when I faint,' I said.

'I will say I did it,' said Bertram. 'Claim I was protecting her.'

'But everyone saw you standing at the altar,' objected

2

Merry.

'She's right,' said Hans. 'It won't wash. Euphemia, you will have to claim he attacked you. Where did you get the knife?'

I blinked at him puzzled.

'Think, girl, think,' said Hans urgently. 'We have only moments to sort your story.'

'It was in his chest,' I said.

'That much is obvious,' said Bertram acerbically. 'But where did you get it from?'

I barely noticed the door opening, nor what was probably the whole congregation attempting to spill into the tiny room. All I could see was Bertram's face.

'Dear God,' I said. 'You cannot believe that *I* did this? Bertram? You know me! You love me! We are to be married.'

But Bertram only shook his head and disappeared among the crowd as they surged forward towards me.

That evening, despite protests from my step-father, the Bishop, I was thrown into the local jail awaiting someone senior to come down from London and take charge of the case. Thrown is perhaps too harsh a word. In truth, the local constabulary, who knew me from living on Hans and Richenda's estate, were as confused as I was. They apologetically took my boots, gloves, stockings, and veil. The sergeant allowed Richenda's kitchen to send down a plate of hot food. That it was a selection of meats from what should have been my wedding breakfast was spoken of by no one.

Hans came and dried my tears. With infinite practicality he brought a hot damp cloth, wrapped in a thick towel, so I could finally clean the blood and fingerprint ink off my hands. He said that Bertram was unavailable. Besides, the police only wanted me to have contact with one person on the outside. 'As I am not related to you, I was preferred,' he explained.

'They all think I did it, don't they?' I said.

'The circumstantial evidence is overwhelming,' said Hans. 'If you will not say that he attacked you…'

'It happened in a church,' I said. 'In God's house. I cannot lie.'

'I was taught to believe that God was everywhere,' said Hans mildly.

'I didn't kill him, Hans.'

'I would very much like to believe that. Tell me what happened.'

'I found him,' I said. 'He was lying there with a knife in him. Behind the wooden screen. You saw it had fallen over?'

Hans nodded. 'It was the sound of that hitting the stone floor that brought us running. I assumed it was a modesty screen for you. To hide your dress if anyone walked in unexpectedly.'

'I do not know. I only know that as I was standing, waiting for the you to come and escort me down the aisle – does the Bishop think that I did it? My mother?'

'Your mother has retired to the guest chamber Richenda allocated her. The Bishop is praying for you.'

'I see,' I said, swallowing hard.

'You were saying?'

'Yes,' I shook the cobwebs away. 'I heard a gurgling sound coming from behind the screen. When I pushed it back, I found Richard lying on the floor, a knife protruding from his chest.'

'He was still alive?'

'Yes.'

4

'What did you do?'

'I knelt down beside him. He merely blinked at me. I could see at once he was beyond my skill. I told him I would fetch help.'

'But you didn't,' said Hans.

'No, he caught my wrist and held it with surprising force for a dying man. He tried to speak but could not utter the words. His lips moved, but... it was horrible.'

Hans put one hand over mine. 'I am sure it was,' he said. 'But why, then, did you not call for help?'

'He motioned to his chest and I realised he wanted me to pull the knife out. So, I did – and then the blood went everywhere.'

'It would,' said Hans. 'Did he say anything then?'

'No. It was the strangest thing. He made a different gurgling sound, akin to a laugh, and then he died.'

Hans sighed deeply and bowed his head.

'I didn't do it, Hans. I swear.'

'I am very much afraid you will not be believed. Not that that man didn't deserve... I've had business dealings with him. He was rotten to the core. Goodness only knows what you endured as a servant in his house.' He shook his head. 'No one will cry at his funeral. I could...' he hesitated.

'What?'

'You are on my land. My men are loyal to me. I could get you away.'

'Run away?'

'You would not be able to come back. And I fear Bertram would not...'

'I see.'

'You know I have always had a fondness for you, Euphemia. I could arrange something. Somewhere for you to live. Perhaps in Scotland, or even on the Continent.' He must have read the expression on my face. 'I do not offer this lightly. I greatly fear that you will be found guilty and hanged. I can offer you a way out. It is not an honourable course, but you will be kept safe and you will not be alone. I will visit and help you build a new life.'

'Are you asking me to be your mistress?'

Hans gave a faint smile. 'My primary concern is to preserve your life. Anything else... is for future consideration. I offer you a way to escape, with no conditions attached.'

I could not find the words to show how deeply he had disappointed me. Instead I dropped my gaze to the lace hem of my dress.

Hans patted my hand. 'I understand,' he said. 'It is a lot to think about. Such a reversal in your fortunes, and on the cusp of your matrimony, is not an easy thing to comprehend. But, Euphemia, you are in real danger. Let me help you. I will leave you now to think on matters. You are a sensible woman. I am confident you will make the right choice. I will return in the morning for your decision. It is already very late, and you must be exhausted.' He lifted my right hand to his lips and kissed it. I said nothing. He called for the local bobby to let him out of the cell. The man came quickly. A clink of keys, footsteps, and I was alone again. I managed to wait until then before hot tears spilled down my face.

Although I could contain my sobs, I could not stop the tears which flowed on and on. I brushed them angrily away. Night drew in. Opposite my cell stood an unmanned desk. I assumed this was to leave me the illusion of privacy, for there was nothing between myself and the open bars of the cell wall. Sanitary amenities were the lowest possible. An oil lantern burned at the empty station, throwing shadows of the bars across the cell. A single high and tiny window let in a sliver of moonlight. I sat in the corner and gazed up through the miniscule opening. Under this moon I should have been in my marriage bed with Bertram. What had Hans had called it? A reversal of my fortune? My chest heaved as I struggled to contain my weeping.

A long shadow blotted out much of the light. 'What an affecting sight!' said a familiar voice. I would have known that Scottish accent anywhere.

I sprang to my feet and ran to the edge of my cage. 'Rory!' I cried. 'Have you come to help me?'

Rory McLeod was Bertram's former factotum, and my old comrade-in-arms from my days at working as a maid at Stapleford Hall. Once, we had been more than that.

'You mean make you an offer like that German, Muller?'

'What? No. Of course not! I... You were listening!'

He was no more than a solid shadow in the dark. I could barely make out the features of his face by the lamplight, but I knew at once that his mood was what I had feared most – one of jealousy and resentment that cast me as a villainess.

'I forgot,' interrupted Rory in an unpleasant tone, 'the likes of me are not good enough for you. Only a gentleman can take your fancy.'

I clasped one cold bar in each hand. 'Bertram's status had nothing to do with my decision to accept his proposal.' My tears had stopped at the sight of what I had thought to be my old friend, but now I began to feel a deep concern. What was it Rory had gone on to do after leaving Bertram's employ? 'You are with the police now?' I asked.

'I am,' said Rory. 'Pure chance that I was in the area. I have just closed another case. Successfully. I believe the perpetrator will hang.'

'And you are here to investigate my case?' I said, trying hard to keep the hope from my voice. Rory might be angry with me, but I knew him to be a fair man. We had worked together on enough cases that I knew he believed in justice.

He moved away for a moment then reappeared with a small stool. 'I have read the report of the local sergeant. He included not only a good description of the scene of the crime, but also some detailed witness statements. For a country policeman, he has done an excellent job.'

Rory sat down on the stool. I stood holding onto the bars. I had little choice. The only furniture in my cell was a low bed, screwed to the floor. 'An excellent job,' he continued. 'There is little more to investigate.'

'You have found who attacked Richard?' I gasped, barely able to believe my ears.

'Oh, Euphemia, I think we both know who killed Richard Stapleford. Do you know, among all your wedding guests, there is not one who believes you to be innocent?'

Chapter Two

Rory's one concession to our previous association was to allow me a blanket. I heard him tell the local sergeant that I was certain not to be one of those prisoners who escaped their fate by suicide. His final words to me were to tell me that he had arranged transport to take me to London, where his chief inspector would also look at my case. However, he told me he expected that I would not be given bail and that the decision would be to move straight to prosecution. When I asked him if he thought I had killed Richard, he gave the first sign of any real emotion and sighed.

'Och, Euphemia,' he said, 'you've changed so much from that bonnie, wee lassie I first knew, I could not say what ye would be capable of now.'

He took the lamp with him when he left, plunging me into darkness. In equal parts exhausted, terrified, and heartsore, I eventually fell asleep, but my pillow was damp with tears.

I awoke the next morning to the sound of jangling keys. I had long learned the trick of awakening without opening my eyes. The key turned in the lock and the door creaked open. Someone came into my cell, but I did not hear the cell door being relocked. Cautiously, I opened one eye.

There, leaning against the back wall of my cell and regarding me with his arms crossed, was the spy I knew as Fitzroy, and more recently by his first name, Eric. We had not parted on good terms, but not exactly on bad terms either. I suppose it may have been called a truce. He had lied to me, and he had, if not directly caused, then at least failed to prevent a tragedy in my family. I understood the decisions he had taken – that way of thinking creeps into your soul when you work for long enough with an agent of the Crown. He did – does – bad things, so that the balance of justice and safety is preserved in the country.

I had thought myself rid of him. I had promised Bertram that I would never see him again. And yet he, of all people, now stood in my cell.

I sat up, pulling the blanket around my blood-stained dress. 'Good morning,' I said.

The spy raised an eyebrow. 'My wedding invitation get lost in the post?'

'We did not exactly part as friends,' I said.

Fitzroy rubbed a hand over his forehead. 'Perhaps not. But I had thought we had reached an understanding. You do not actually hate me at this moment, do you?'

'No,' I said.

Fitzroy pushed away from the walk and began to pace the cell. 'Mind you, I might have taken my welcome for granted and attended your ceremony anyway if I thought it was going to be this interesting.' He paused to look at me. A frown briefly passed over his brow. Then he began to pace again. 'You never do things the easy way, do you, Euphemia?'

'I didn't kill him!' I cried, rising to my feet.

Fitzroy didn't even pause in his pacing. He merely batted my statement away with his left hand. 'Oh, I know that,' he said.

I came forward, dropping the blanket to clutch on his sleeve and stop him from moving. 'They have found the killer?' I stared up into his face. I noticed he was unshaven and there were shadows around his eyes. He frowned down at me.

'No, I don't believe so. Even in the country they normally let one person out when they accuse another, don't they?'

'I don't understand,' I said. 'How do you know I didn't do it?'

The frown deepened. 'Because I know you,' said the spy. 'I'm well aware that you believe in justice, and Lord knows if any man deserved to feel the dagger of justice in his heart, it was Richard Stapleford. But you would never take it upon yourself to do so - and in a house of God to boot? You've got vicar's daughter written through you as clearly as if you were a stick of Brighton rock. This was a vicious, hate-filled attack – not your style at all.'

I prevented him from continuing by throwing my arms around his neck and sobbing loudly into his shoulder. Although he always claims he is no gentleman, Fitzroy did as any gentleman might in such circumstances: he froze in horror. To his credit he did not push me away.

I released him and looked up. 'Everyone else believes me to be guilty,' I said, the tears rolling once more down my face. 'My mother, the Bishop, probably even little J-J-Joe.'

'Bertram believed you, did he not?'

My voice dropped to a whisper. 'No. He said so at the time. He turned away from me.' My voice broke on this last sentence and I bowed my head. 'I am sorry,' I said. 'I do not appear able to stop weeping.'

Fitzroy stepped towards me and placed his hands on my shoulders. He leaned forward and his breath was warm against my ear. 'I am here. You are safe.'

He turned me round and pushed me gently me out of the cell, sitting me down behind the desk. He swept the papers off it onto the floor and sat on the edge of it, looking down at me. 'I am sorry,' he said. 'I would have been here earlier, but the news of your arrest only reached me in the early hours of the morning. I would not have had you spend the night in a cell if I could have avoided it.'

'Rory and Hans both said I will hang,' I said. I had to clutch my hands together to stop them trembling. 'This all feels like a nightmare. I keep thinking I will wake up.'

'Well, you won't hang, and you won't spend another moment behind bars.'

'But Rory,' I said.

'You can leave me to deal with McLeod,' said the spy, his face grim. 'I don't take kindly to anyone mistreating one of my assets.'

'But what can you do?'

'Ah, now this is the bit I wanted you to sit down for. There are a couple of options to consider. Do you want me to get you some breakfast first? Coffee?'

I shook my head. 'I would be sick,' I said.

'Let's avoid that, shall we? I am in need of a shave and a bath as it is, but I would rather not make my unkempt condition worse.'

'At least you are not wearing clothing covered in blood. My wedding dress…' My voice broke and tears started to fall again.

He reached over and passed me a clean handkerchief. His voice softened slightly. 'I need you to stop crying, Euphemia. I can see how distressed you are, and I understand why, but we have some serious decisions to make. I need you to be fully conscious of the choices at hand.'

'I'm sorry,' I said. 'It's all so awful…'

'C'mon, Euphemia. You're stronger than this. I promised that no further harm will come to you. Do you trust me or not?'

For the first time in over twenty-four hours I smiled.

Fitzroy smiled wryly back at me.

'Thank you,' I said. 'What do I need to do?'

He leant forward and briefly brushed my hand. 'Good girl. Oh, by the by, I met Hans on my way here. He told me of the offer he had made you…'

'He told you?'

Fitzroy shrugged. 'I gave him a little encouragement. Then I declined on your behalf.'

'Thank you,' I said.

'Don't think too badly of him. It might have been a most ungentlemanly offer, but it wasn't made without, I suspect, some affection and genuine desire for your well-being. He would have been putting himself at some risk. Especially if he believes you to be guilty. If you had both been caught, he would likely have hanged alongside you. Besides, you always liked him, didn't you? If he'd known you were an heiress, he'd have married you rather than Richenda.'

'How delightful you make him sound.'

'That's more like my Euphemia. Now, of the options I am offering you, my last resort is to get you out of the country. Alas, I would not be setting you up in some bijou chateau, but rather lodging you with some very ordinary French folk who owe me a favour. Of course, you would not be able to return to England until the real killer has been caught. In the normal way of things, I'd be more than happy to take that on, but as the reality of war with Germany comes closer, I will have other calls upon my time. I might not be able to devote as much time as is needed before war is upon us, and then solving this crime would become even more difficult. To be frank, I also don't like the idea of you being out of England when the war begins. I have… well, never mind that. It wouldn't be my first preference for you.'

I nodded. 'I dreamed – when we were in the Highlands –

about what is to come. I don't normally believe in omens, but having met Madame Arcana…'

'She might do work for the nation, but she's a charlatan.'

I shook my head. 'Not all the time… however, I agree this is not the best option. What are the others?'

'There is really only one other viable option,' said the spy. 'And you're not going to like it. It would mean spending a great deal more time with me.'

'You said no chateau…'

'No, no. I don't mean in a romantic sense,' said Fitzroy curtly. 'I'm no Hans Muller, trying to take advantage of a woman in dire circumstances.'

'I'm sorry,' I said, blushing furiously. 'It feels like so many people have let me down…'

'We all have lines we will not cross, even I,' said the spy sounding slightly ruffled. He smoothed down his hair and fiddled with cuff in a most un-Fitzroy manner. Then he added, 'Unless I was ordered to do so,' in a low voice. His head was down, avoiding my gaze. I chose to pretend that I had not heard his addendum.

'I am sorry,' I repeated.

'Yes, well, never mind. Have you ever seen one of these?' He produced a small, triangular badge from his pocket. It was black with some curious sigils enamelled in white.

'Is it a good luck charm?'

Fitzroy threw back his head and roared with laughter. When he had recovered himself, he put the badge back in his pocket and wiped tears of amusement from his eyes with the back of his hand.[1]

'Oh, Euphemia, even in the direst straits you make me

---

[1] A gentleman would have used a handkerchief.

14

laugh! Can you see me with a good luck charm?'

'No. I imagine you believe you make your own fortune.'

'To some extent. It's an insignia.'

'Of what?'

'Of authority. All agents of the crown carry these.'

'Oh.'

'It allows us a certain licence, but it also demands a level of duty that you have never been asked to undertake.'

'You've made me choose between saving my relatives and following your orders!'

The spy nodded. 'Yes, but if you carry one of these, there is no choice in the matter. Duty to the Crown supersedes all. You've seen me bend the rules on more than one occasion, but I've never broken them. In the final instance, I am no one's son, no one's father, no one's friend and no one's brother. I am an Agent of the Crown.'

'That is quite a burden.'

'I am glad you recognise that,' said Fitzroy.

'It's why you said you'd never marry, isn't it?'

Fitzroy nodded. 'But you are to marry Bertram.'

'That is by no means a certain thing. Not now.'

'Oh, it will be,' said Fitzroy with a certain grimness.

'You will not force him to marry me,' I said. The spy grunted noncommittally. 'I'm serious, Fitzroy. I want no unwilling bridegroom.'

'The man's a fool in many ways, but he loves you.'

'So says the confirmed bachelor!'

Fitzroy flashed me a wicked grin. 'I never said I lived like a monk. I know something of relationships – and the need for them. Especially in this line of work. As a man, I have far more options open to me than marriage. You, however, don't.'

I felt the blood creeping into my cheeks. 'Interesting as

all this may be,' I said, in an attempt to change topic, 'but what has this all to do with my current situation?'

Fitzroy gave me a disbelieving look.[2] 'Work it out.'

I thought for a few moments then the truth gradually dawned on me. I looked up and saw the spy was trying not to laugh. 'Really? You find my consternation amusing?'

He shrugged. 'Your expression, as they say, is worthy of a picture.'

'You're offering me the chance to become an Agent of the Crown? You can do that?'

'I can swear you in here and now. You will walk out of the door a free woman.'

'And then?' I asked.

'If we can, I suggest we solve this murder in the next forty-eight hours – for your sake. I assume you don't want your friends and family believing you to be a killer?'

'Why forty-eight hours?'

'Because that is likely all the time we will be able to spare before other duties demand our attention.'

'The war?' I said.

Now very sober and grim, Fitzroy nodded.

'I see. My two options are to retreat to France or become an Agent of the Crown?'

'We could see France as a temporary measure, until something better came up,' said Fitzroy.

'Like?'

'Someone unmasking the real murderer.'

'But I'd still have run away,' I said.

'You would have put that aside too,' said Fitzroy.

---

[2]Both eyebrows raised instead of the one. He isn't the most communicative when it comes to facial expressions, but even by then I had learned to read him to an adequate degree.

'What?'

'Your sense of honour. While you work with me, I will do my best to ensure you are not put into a situation that is too morally demanding for you, but you must accept you may not always be working with me.'

'If I marry?'

'It makes no difference to your oath.'

'So, I would have to face those choices that you deliberately ruled out?'

'Possibly, but if your family is a low profile one that lives out of London, we should be able to keep them at a distance to your other activities.'

'I could not tell them?'

Fitzroy shook his head. 'You can tell one person. I recommend telling any husband you take, after you are married –'

'You mean in case they jilt me?'

Fitzroy coughed. 'I seem to remember it is generally you who do the jilting. How many times have been engaged, Euphemia?'

'Touché,' I said. 'I do not have the most successful of romantic records.'

'Oh, I don't know. Having people tumble into love with you all the time must be quite entertaining.'

'So, until I marry Bertram, I couldn't tell him, even though he's signed the Official Secrets Act?'

'No.'

'I don't suppose you would consider recruiting him?'

Fitzroy made an odd noise somewhere between a chuckle and a cough. 'Honestly, Euphemia, your naivety can be amusing, but this is not the place for it. The Service is not some kind of social tea-taking club. We consider many people but recruit very few. That I am recruiting you, or offering to, is akin to a minor miracle in terms of the department's history.'

'And Bertram?'

'No.'

'But -'

'We are a military service and Bertram's heart condition makes him unfit to be enlisted. Besides, he has no unique talent to offer that would take him over the line from asset to agent, even if he were healthy.'

This last speech was delivered in a flat, merciless tone and it gave me pause, as Fitzroy intended.

'I take it my unique talent is my sex?'

'Partly, but not entirely. You also have a first-class brain, as well as an innately adventurous nature – you are capable of being merciless when required. That is your most rare talent.'

I started as if he had struck me.

'You have, have you not, watched me shoot more than one man to death? Indeed, on more than one occasion you have encouraged me to execute a person who might not otherwise have been subject to justice.'

'You make me sound bloodthirsty,' I said. I could feel bile rising in my throat at this description of me.

Fitzroy shook his head. 'Not at all. If you were, it would make you most unsuitable. However, you have come to terms with understanding that justice and necessity are cruel partners in this line of work.' He gave an almost imperceptible sigh. 'I know I make the service look very glamorous and adventurous, but that is my personal charisma. The job is often dirty and frequently harsh on an agent.' He gave me his wry grin. 'Am I selling you this?'

'No,' I said. 'And it has taken me some moments to realise what you are doing, because I do not think I have

18

ever seen you do it before.'

This time the eyebrow raised was an enquiring one.

'Be totally honest,' I said.

Fitzroy gave a crack of laughter. 'Touché,' he said. 'Are you in?'

'Yes,' I said, and so began my service to our country as an Agent of the Crown.

Chapter Three

He swore me in right there and then.[3] I remember my voice shook as I repeated the words. It was not the strong, steady avowal I would have liked to have made. Later, he told me that if it had been, he would have worried that I did not understand what I was getting myself into.

Not long after this, almost as if he had timed it to perfection, Merry arrived with a bag of my clothes. Fitzroy left while she helped me to change into the least favourite of my dresses. My skin still bore traces of my interaction with Richard and would until I enjoyed the comfort of a hot bath.

'Do you know where you are going?' Merry asked as she did up the last of my buttons.

'No,' I said.

''E said 'ow I was not to ask you questions, but I hope you know what you're doing, Euphemia. Can you trust this special policeman? 'E could be taking you off to Gawd knows where.'

I turned to face her and took her hands in my own. 'I can trust him. Thank you for coming to me.'

'You know 'ow I'd do anything for you,' said Merry. 'Even if you had killed that bas – that bad man.'

'I thought everyone believed I had done it?' I said.

'Both believed and not believed, if you ask me,' said Merry. 'Mr Bertram is right worked up. 'E…'

'Mistress Merrit, I thought we had agreed there would be no chatter?' said Fitzroy, coming back into the room. 'Your

---

[3] I can't give you details of the oath. I'm sure you understand why.

20

help is very much appreciated. If there is anything more you can do to help, I will be in touch, but now Euphemia and I must leave.' He offered me his arm. I took it. It felt strange to be standing thus with him. I had taken both Rory's and Bertram's arms on occasion. Even Hans', but I had never imagined I would be in such close proximity to the spy. It felt like crossing a line into another world. I also could not help but notice, for all his protestations of his being a far from glamorous position, that his jacket was both well-cut and of the finest cloth. I wondered if, now I was an agent, I would be paid? Possibly I would be able to support myself without resorting to marriage?[4] Merry broke in on my thoughts.

'What do I do with this?' she asked holding up my wedding dress.

'Burn it,' said Fitzroy and I as one. Merry looked a little taken aback. Then, to my surprise, she bobbed a slight curtsey. Fitzroy touched the brim of his hat to her and walked away. As I was holding his arm, I was also carried off before I could say goodbye.

'Are you using her as an asset?' I asked.

'I had thought about it,' said Fitzroy. 'However, her location, as well as her condition, makes me doubt her usefulness.'

'Condition?'

He looked down at me. 'Did you not notice she is with child? Her hair? Her skin? Her expanded waist-line? The mints she keeps sucking?'

I looked down at my feet as the blood rushed into my face. This was not the kind of thing one discussed with a person of the opposite sex.

---

[4] I could not believe Bertram would want me back.

'You no longer have the luxury of being prudish,' said Fitzroy. Then I felt him stiffen slightly. 'Damn, I had hoped to spare you this. Follow my lead.'

I looked up and saw Rory McLeod striding towards us. 'What the hell is the meaning of this?' he shouted.

Fitzroy stopped to meet him and showed him the small emblem he had shown me earlier. 'I know what you are,' sneered Rory. 'But you have no right to take this woman from her cell. She is not above the law.'

'Show him, Euphemia,' said Fitzroy softly to me.

I took the identical badge from my pocket and showed it wordlessly to Rory.

'Good God,' he said. 'I should have known. You wrap every man who crosses your path around your finger. I would have thought at least you would have been immune to that, Fitzroy.'

'Oh, I am,' said the spy. 'Euphemia's recruitment has been planned for some time by my superiors. Your actions merely brought that day forward a little.'

'If I believed that for a moment,' said Rory, 'I would wish God's mercy on her. But I don't. You've had your eye on her from the beginning. I know why you want her.' His eyes looked me over from top to toe. 'She caught me the same way, once.'

'You overestimate my rank,' said Fitzroy in a mild voice. 'I do not determine who is to be recruited.' His tone might be soft, but I could feel the muscles tensing in his arm under my hand. I got the distinct impression he wanted to punch Rory in the face. However, outwardly he remained calm. 'How is the position, by the way? Are you enjoying being an agent of the law? Do you find the police suits you?' A look passed between them that I could not interpret.

'If war comes, I will enlist. I want nothing to do with you

or yours.'

'Very noble, I'm sure,' said Fitzroy. 'Now, if you will excuse us, we have somewhere to be.'

'I could summon -'

The spy cut him off. 'You could summon all kinds of people, but you know the rules, you have to let her go. Let's avoid any more unpleasantness, shall we?' The latter sentence sounded to my ears clearly a threat. Rory must have thought so too, because with a noise not unlike a snarl, he stepped aside.

Once we were out of earshot, Fitzroy commented, 'I did warn you not to get involved with him. He has a streak of jealousy and a desire to possess and control that is bound to sabotage any relationship with all but the meekest of women.'

'Did you get him his job? Did he come to you when he left Bertram?'

'Yes, and yes. He also believes he is still in love with you and hates both himself and you for it.'

'That much I had worked out for myself. Where are we going? And how do we get there?'

'As for where, you will find out. As for how, we will use my motor car. I haven't had it long and have been keen to give it a good run. I hope that hat is tied on securely.'

Fitzroy's style of driving certainly proved adventurous. The speed of the night air passing us negated any ability to communicate and more than once I found myself gripping the side of my seat. The spy drove with a curiously calm expression on his face. I eventually worked out that he was enjoying himself no end.

We arrived in the outskirts of London as dawn broke. He pulled into a mews lane and stopped outside a building that showed recent signs of renovation. A smart two-storey dwelling, it stood at the end of the mews next to a walled area. Fitzroy turned off the engine and jumped out. He appeared at my side to help me down.

'You're trembling,' he said.

'Shivering,' I corrected. 'I am cold.'

'Tea, an open fire, and then a hot bath,' said Fitzroy. 'In that order. We don't want you getting hypothermia.'

'Is this your home?' I asked as he put a key to the front door. 'Do you have servants?'

'Not exactly my home. A little place I use from time to time. And no, I don't have servants.'

I followed him across the threshold feeling more than a little wary. We entered a small, dark lobby. He shut the door behind us and bolted it. Then he turned up a gas lamp on the wall. I could now see a long mirror hung on one wall, a small chest of drawers beneath it. Then I noticed a gun hanging in a neat holster on the wall next to a coat stand.

'Shouldn't we have stayed at the Muller estate to search for clues?' I said, trying very hard not to fixate on the gun. Fitzroy shrugged himself out of his coat and hung it up. He shook his head.

'I had a look over the place myself. Nothing to see. No, this will be much more about people, and those who had a grudge against Richard. Coat? You can take your hat off in front of the mirror.' I handed him my coat and, all too conscious of his proximity, took my hat off and pulled my hair into some shape.

'A lot of people,' I said, as calmly as I could, and as if I was used to taking my hat off in front of men.[5]

'Unfortunately, I agree. Come through to the lounge and I will light the fire. You're looking blue at the edges. My driving didn't frighten you, did it?'

'It was enlivening,' I said following him through the door.[6] Fitzroy gave a grin that was positively boyish.

'I had one lady faint on me,' he said. 'Fortunately, I had secured her in her seat as I was afraid such a thing might occur.'

'But you were not so with me?'

'No,' he said, the grin still on his face. 'I was more afraid you would ask me to show you how to drive.'

'I thought of asking,' I said, trying to follow his joking manner.

'Oh, I'll teach you,' said Fitzroy. 'It will be a useful skill. Now, sit.'

I sat obediently down in a leather armchair and began to take in my surroundings. He lit the fire and two lamps then left me. I could hear him in the next room whistling. This, alone, was most unnerving. The lounge, as he had termed it, was a medium-sized room that must once have been the original stabling for a carriage. It had been panelled with a dark wood, and thick red carpet laid on the floor. The windows remained hidden behind wooden shutters. A chimney had been inset and a hearth of suitable size roared out a welcoming heat. The room contained two leather wing-backed armchairs, a desk (clear of papers) with a globe on top of it, and a small table set beside the chairs which faced the fire. There were also some other low furnishings with

---

[5]No lady should be. A hat is something to be removed in the privacy of one's own room, and if anyone is present it should only be one's lady's maid.

[6]Yes, a gentleman would have let me go first.

closed doors, the use of which I could not guess. A single picture hung above the fireplace, of a young, rather beautiful, red-haired woman, who smiled wistfully down at me. For some reason her expression struck me as one of someone hiding many secrets. The portrait was head and shoulders only, and the brief outline of her blue dress gave no clue as to the era. However, around her neck she wore a formidable string of diamonds, such as is rarely seen today.

A few moments later he returned carrying a tray on which there were two teacups and saucers and a decanter. He had taken off his jacket, although he still wore his waistcoat. Even Bertram had never let me see him in shirtsleeves.

'My bag...' I began.

'It'll be safe enough in the car for now,' he said, setting down the tray. 'I've put milk and sugar in your tea. I'm having an extra kick in mine.' He looked at me for a moment. 'You had better have one too. It's been a long day for you.' Before I could protest, he poured a large dash from the decanter into both cups and passed one to me. Then he sat down in the chair beside me and stretched out his legs to the fire. He took a sip from his tea cup and closed his eyes.

'I saw you admiring my picture,' he said, making me jump.

'She's very beautiful,' I said.

Fitzroy opened his eyes again. 'Yes, she is.'

I waited, but he didn't say anything else. Finally, my curiosity overcame me. 'Who is she?'

The spy smiled. 'My mother. She died when I was twelve.'

'I am sorry. You did not inherit her flaming hair? Just as well in your profession.'

'Oh, I did. I dye it. You're quite right. It does make me stand out otherwise.'

I drank some tea and spluttered. 'This is rather strong.'

'It will do you good.' Fitzroy sat up and turned to me. 'Poor Euphemia, it's all rather through the looking glass for you, isn't it? Ah, yes, that fits. I'll call you Alice.'

'I beg your pardon.'

'We don't use our real names when we're in the field. I don't object to you calling me Eric in private. It's pleasant to hear my real name spoken. Rarely happens. But you need an operative name too – Alice suits you.'

'Do I get any say in this?'

'No.'

'And I call you Fitzroy? Not the White Rabbit?'

He chuckled. 'You mean because I'm always late from your perspective?'

'Exactly,' I said, somewhat startled he had been so acute.

'Come on, drink up. You can help me get something sorted in the kitchen. Then while it's in the oven we can sort out your bath.'

'You can cook?'

'Naturally. It's a necessary life-skill to be able to feed yourself. You should see what I can conjure up over a bonfire. There's a neat little kitchen through the back.'

When I had finished my tea, I rose feeling a trifle woozy and followed him through the kitchen. He passed me a knife and some carrots. 'Here, chop these, over there.'

I began to do so, when I heard him say my name in tones of shock.

'What?' I asked.

'That is no way to hold a knife,' said the spy emphatically . 'Here, let me show you.'

The next morning, I awoke to the wonderful smell of frying bacon. I sat up in bed and tried to remember exactly where I was. As I took in the little guest room, it all came back. Richard, the jail, and the unusual terms of my liberty. I also remembered sitting by the fire late into the night to allow my hair to dry, while Fitzroy told me about his first pet – a cat, one he had stolen away from the kitchen and taught to walk alongside him when he ventured into the grounds at his home. I had a good idea where those grounds had been from having been prematurely appointed his executor, but he refused to elaborate. As I hurried to get dressed, I reflected that I had felt remarkably easy in his company. I realised he had been at pains not to treat me as a lady but like, I presumed, a comrade. However, given the dire straits of my situation I found that I was thinking of him in terms that I might an older brother, if I had had one, who had come to straighten out all my problems. Things, I decided as I headed down the stairs, could have been far worse. All in all, I was grateful to him and rather excited about what my future might hold. I did my best to ignore the hole in my heart where my relationship with Bertram had resided.

I went through to the small table in the kitchen where we had eaten last night and found Fitzroy, again in his shirt sleeves, laying out bacon, scrambled eggs, and toast. 'Coffee's on the stove,' he said. 'Should be ready any moment. Don't expect this sort of service in general.'

'I will wash the dishes.'

'Do you know how?'

'I used to be a maid, remember?'

He gave me a charming smile. 'But were you any good?'

'Absolutely rubbish,' I said sitting down. 'But Merry taught me well.'

'I like Merry,' said Fitzroy, 'and as you know I don't generally like people.'

'She's very practical and can keep her head in a crisis.'

Fitzroy nodded, and spoke through a mouthful of egg, 'Don't suppose there's any chance of her moving to the metropolis?'

'I think she and Merritt are settled on Bertram's estate. Besides, you said she was pregnant. Although I barely noticed any difference in her waistline.'

'You don't look properly,' said Fitzroy, spearing a slice of bacon with his fork. 'Besides, she won't be pregnant for ever. I believe nine months is the usual term.'

I felt myself blushing again and leaned over my plate.

'Really, Euphemia, you need to harden up. We will have to discuss more intimate subjects than this on occasion. The work requires it.'

'Being through the looking glass is an adjustment,' I said. 'I mean, learning you actually have red hair, seeing you in your shirt sleeves at breakfast, not to mention experiencing your unique style of driving.'

Fitzroy chuckled with appreciation. 'Poor Alice,' he said. 'I do appreciate you not making a fuss about staying here. Most ladies would have gone into histrionics.'

I smiled at him. 'I trust you,' I said without thinking, and found that I did.

Fitzroy's expression became serious. 'Thank you,' he said quietly. 'I shall endeavour to live up to your opinion.'

'And I shall try to keep it as manageably low as possible for you,' I retorted.

He laughed. 'Now, if it won't put you off your breakfast, could you please go through exactly what happened in the church with Richard and afterwards up till the point I arrived.'

I told him in as much detail as I could remember. He listened without interrupting. When I had finished, he poured me more coffee. 'Firstly, I should tell you that you probably did kill Stapleford.' He held up his hand before I could protest. 'An instrument that has caused a puncturing wound has to be removed in a certain way or fatal blood loss will occur. While it stays in it actually prevents blood loss. As soon as you pull it out the wound opens fully, and the victim bleeds out at once without immediate medical attention. Way beyond your skills. No court in the land would convict you, but I'd like you to remember this in case you are ever tempted to pull a knife or some such thing out of me. You will be trained in some basic medical techniques, but in the meantime remember that!'

'He wanted me to pull it out,' I said, confused.

'Yes, I noticed that. I think we will find that the wound – I had a brief look at the body – would have been mortal anyway, so I wouldn't feel bad about it. Interesting though, the sound you said he made when you removed the blade.'

'The gurgling or the laugh?'

'The gurgling is quite normal,' said Fitzroy with a flash of a smile. 'I meant the laugh.'

'He wanted me to be caught with the knife in my hand, didn't he?'

'I believe so. Which begs the question: who could have done this deed that he cared so little about their arrest that he would rather his death was attributed to you?'

'You mean it might have been someone he cared about?'

'Richenda, for example. I believe the bond between twins is strong.'

'She was witnessed in the church at the time.'

'We need to check through the witness statements to rule out the possibility of her slipping out to stab him and then reappearing in the church. You were on her home ground. If there was a short cut, she would have known it.'

'Richenda does not exactly have a personage that can slip

by unnoticed.'

Fitzroy choked slightly on his bacon. 'Don't make me laugh while I'm eating!' He swallowed a swig of coffee. 'I also noted that Hans said he had had bad dealings with Richard – and he wanted to rescue you as well. I have a mark against his name. I suppose the real question is, how much did Richard hate you? Who would he let get off scot-free if he could attribute his own murder to you?'

I considered the question carefully. 'The issue is,' I said, 'that Richard did not seem to be a normal man.' Fitzroy gave me his two-raised-eyebrows look of mock astonishment and continued eating. 'I mean that while I might be able to fathom what gentlemen of my general acquaintance might do, Richard's way of thinking was unlike anything I have come across before.'

Fitzroy lowered his eyebrows and waved his fork in a continue-type gesture.

'I thought he had some fondness for Richenda, but after the episode where he abducted and threatened her children…'

Fitzroy swallowed loudly and said, 'You believe he did so, but have no proof.'

'You think so too.'

'Immaterial. Stick to facts.'

'According to Richenda, he never intervened for her when she was estranged from their father.'

'Better, but you only have Richenda's word. Is she reliable?'

I took a deep breath. 'Alright. Richenda when I first met her was self-centred, occasionally cruel, and willing to turn a blind eye to much of what her twin did – including the way he treated staff. Since she left the household she has changed almost beyond recognition. I would not suggest hers is a happy marriage, but her attitude towards me and even her servants has changed. She is no longer so selfish. She does her best to think of others, especially her children.'

'But she left you to run her household.'

'True, but she was not trained to. I was.'

'You are suggesting that her aversion has its root cause in fear?' said Fitzroy.

'I did not consider that. But it would fit. She would be afraid of letting people down and appearing foolish. But my primary argument is that, away from Richard, she became a much more thoughtful and considerate person. Living with him, it was as if he controlled her. She acquiesced to all his demands.'

Fitzroy nodded. 'In his business dealings he was known for wanting complete control. He preferred to engender fear over loyalty.'

'You mean he blackmailed people?'

Fitzroy began eating again and repeated the annoying fork gesture. I watched my breakfast grow cold. 'In my interactions with him, I found him unkind, but not stupidly so. Merry, having been with the household since she was very young, was something of a favourite, and he never treated her badly.'

'So, he knew how to plan the game? He was intelligent and could interpret social situations.'

'Mostly. Sometimes he spoke shockingly, such as when he spoke of his new wife when I was in Ghent.'

'What did he say?'

'It was quite crude.'

Fitzroy sighed in exasperation.

'He said that he was keeping his wife on her back so as to ensure an heir.'

'Kind of thing many gentlemen might say at a Club,' said

Fitzroy. I heard the scorn behind the word 'gentlemen'.

'I wouldn't know, but it was not what I would expect a gentleman to say in front of ladies in a public area.'

Fitzroy shrugged. 'Perhaps he was trying to shock you.'

'At the time it appeared more of an off-the-cuff comment. There was a warning implicit to Bertram that he intended to inherit Stapleford Hall.'

'Control and ownership,' said Fitzroy.

'He showed no remorse when either of his parents died. Nor his cousin. Nor his supposed best friend.'

'You thought he killed Baggy Tipton, didn't you?'

'But I never had any evidence that wasn't circumstantial.'

'Agreed. In predicting past or previous behaviour the key is to ensure that you are basing your conclusions on facts. Believing you know something without examining it for proof is the best way to fool yourself.'

'But you agree Richard was a megalomaniac, narcissistic, amoral creature?'

'Interesting you say amoral, but yes, overall I am inclined to agree. My observations suggest that he felt no need to play by the usual rules of society and felt no regret when he broke them,' said Fitzroy.

'He acted as if they should not apply to him,' I said. 'Does that mean he was mad?'

Fitzroy wiped his plate clean with a piece of toast. 'That doesn't concern me. I am only interested in what he has done, and what he might have done if still alive.'

'He was evil.'

Fitzroy cocked his head to one side. 'That is not a very helpful descriptor in our business. It's the value of an individual in preserving our country and our way of life that has to be our foremost concern.'

'Arms and banking,' I said. My stomach churned and I

regretted the little breakfast I had eaten.

'Certainly if Richard Stapleford had been a greengrocer, the local authorities would have swept him up before.' He gulped down a last mouthful of coffee. 'But he would not have been of any interest to us. Now, Euphemia, the clock is ticking on that forty-eight hours. I have copies of the witness statements and a decent plan of the estate. We need to establish who could have been in the antechamber before you and who had a reason to kill Richard Stapleford. My somewhat forlorn hope is that we will catch an obvious overlap.'

'But you think this is a long shot?'

'Over the hills and far away. I think we will be lucky if we find one person in your wedding congregation that liked the man. I have partial backgrounds for some of the guests. I am hoping you can fill in the rest.'

'I will do my best.'

'I expect no less. Now, come through to the lounge and I will introduce you to the exciting world of intelligence.' He grinned as he said this. I must have looked wary for he continued, 'You'll see what I mean.'

Chapter Four

Five hours later my head spun, and my neck hurt as if a yoke had been laid across it. I looked up from my notes. Fitzroy sat at the other end of the desk working methodically through half of the statements. Between us lay a map of the Muller estate. 'I am on my last statement,' I said.

Fitzroy looked up and for a moment it seemed as if his eyes did not focus on me. 'Good. So am I. We will swap statements and exchange notes. See if we can see something the other has missed.'

'Do you think we could possibly have some coffee or tea?' I ventured.

The spy frowned. The shutters remained closed and the dim light of the lamps made my head ache. Without thinking I massaged the skin around my eyes and my temples. Fitzroy pulled his pocket watch from his waistcoat[7] and flipped open the hunter. 'I suppose we have been at this a while,' he said. 'I tend to lose track of time when I'm working, but I'm used to it. Why don't you make us some soup? There's stuff in the kitchen.' He gave a slight smile. 'Seems only fair, seeing as I made breakfast.'

'Of course,' I said standing. I now realised how sore my back was. At least in the kitchen I would be able to stretch my tired muscles. Making soup could not be that hard. Essentially, it was no more than foodstuffs in water. I went through to the kitchen. I raided the cupboards and found some basic supplies. I piled together carrots, potatoes, rice

---

[7]Yet again he was jacketless in my presence.

(to make it thicker), tomatoes (I knew many soups were red or brown), a herb (at least I was pretty sure it was a herb, or why else would it be in the kitchen?) and some cheese (for flavour). Then I turned my attention to how the stove might be lit. A small neat thing, the device was obviously very modern. I studied it looking for where I might stick a flame.

'You don't have a clue, do you?' said Fitzroy's voice from behind me. I started and dropped the lit taper in my hand. Fitzroy stamped on it. 'I presume Mrs Deighton never asked you to do more than chop a few vegetables?'

'Not even that. Although I did sometimes sit in the kitchen while she worked.'

Fitzroy blinked at me. 'I suppose that explains last night.' He sighed. 'I didn't realise I would have to teach you everything. This is going to be a very long day.'

I could feel myself blushing. I knew I was not without talents, but at that moment under his mocking stare my mind went completely blank.

'Get an onion and chop it. You do know what an onion is, don't you?'

The resulting soup tasted good despite my help. He showed me a quick and easy method and followed it up by showing me how to toast bread. 'I am not a total idiot,' I said stung.

'No, but you have been spoilt by the life you've led.'

'As a maid?'

'As someone who has rarely had to do anything for herself.'

'I didn't realise that basic cookery skills were needed as an agent of the Crown. Perhaps Merry would have been a better choice,' I said.

I regretted the words the minute they were out of my mouth. Before I could apologise Fitzroy retorted, 'You forget yourself. We are working, Alice, and I am your superior officer. This is a military service. You will never speak to me again like that when we are engaged on business. Do I make myself clear?' He did not raise his voice, but he spoke in a cold, clipped manner. His face bore no expression, but his eyes were dark and flat. For the first time in our acquaintance I felt afraid of him.

'I am sorry. I spoke without thinking. It was unforgivable. After all you...'

He raised a hand, cutting me off. 'We will not speak of this again.' I bowed my head. We sat at the kitchen table in silence. Then we went back through and began working on each other's notes. Fitzroy neither spoke to me nor acknowledged me in any way for several hours. To be so completely ignored, I found surprisingly painful. Fitzroy had been the only person who believed in my innocence and now I felt completely alone. I had just enough pride to keep back my tears.

'I'm still working on it, aren't I?'

I looked up to find him watching me.

'There is no need to look so doleful simply because I set boundaries in our working relationship. If I had thought you were hopeless, I would hardly waste the rest of the day working on all this.'

I had an impulse to leave my seat and rush to hug him, but I did not dare to imagine what response this would bring on when a few ill-judged words had cost me an afternoon of silence.

'Thank you,' I said.

Fitzroy nodded. 'Now, finish that last statement. Then we should eat and come back to this whole mess with fresh eyes.'

'Yes,' I said obediently.

'I'll cook,' said the spy. 'I'm too hungry to take the time to give you another lesson.'

We were halfway through a silent meal when Fitzroy said, 'Don't sulk, Alice. We don't have time for it. From what I've read we're not opening up any promising leads.'

I bit my tongue. I wanted to say I thought he was sulking as much as I was. I wanted to say I thought he was being very heavy-handed, but what I actually said was, 'It isn't my intention to sulk, but rather that I am unsure what to say – how to interact with you in my new position.' I thought about adding 'sir' at the end but doubted I could do so without being sarcastic.

Fitzroy ran his hand through his hair; a sure sign he was feeling exasperated. 'I know. The relationship between handler and asset is much more informal. An asset, although we call on their duty to their country, is essentially doing us a favour. We have no power to stop them walking away. It is normal to act towards them with a degree of friendliness that you would not find between working agents.'

'I see,' I said.

Fitzroy shook his head. 'No, you don't, and I regret circumstances do not allow a longer period of adjustment. If things progress as they should you will shortly be meeting other agents and you need to behave in an appropriate and professional manner. Not only because you are that rare commodity, a female spy – and some of my comrades abhor this idea and will be looking for fault – but because the people you will be meeting may all in their way be exceptional, but none of them have been acquired due to the pleasantness of their personality nor, in some cases, their evenness of temper. In short, agents of the Crown are dangerous people, playing a dangerous game, and you are shockingly naïve.'

'If I had not been facing a murder accusation would you have recruited me?'

Fitzroy was silent for a while. 'Honestly, I am unsure. I would have tested your aptitude for this work to a greater degree and then made my judgement. But circumstances did not allow that, and we have to deal with where we are and what we have.'

'So, I am to treat you as my superior?'

'I would hope I had won your respect over the time we have known each other. I expect respect, dedication, an application to the work that is intense and near all-consuming, and that, in critical situations, you obey me without question. At other times, but not in front of other people, you may respectfully question my decisions if you have sufficient reason to do so. Until your training is complete, I am your instructor and responsible for you.'

At this point I would have previously pointed out that it would have helped matters if this has been explained to me at the start, but I could not think of a way of phrasing it that would not sound rude. I looked up to see the spy still watching me. 'I am aware you are thinking I could have spelled this out earlier, but generally I find that learning occurs better through experience than lecture for most. Besides, you were in no emotional state to take it all in.'

'You mean that we are no longer friends?' I blurted. 'That the previous way we interacted was merely an example of how to handle an asset?'

Fitzroy frowned.

'I am sorry,' I said. 'I -'

He held up his hand to stop me. 'Of course we are friends. You began as an asset, but for heaven's sake, I made you my executor. I have trusted you with details of my background – I have trusted you more than anyone I have worked with in the past ten years.' He leaned forward over the table, 'But we cannot be friends, or act as friends, when we are working. There is no room for emotion. Do you understand?'

I shook my head. 'But I will try to.'

'Good, now eat up and stop looking so goddamn forlorn. It's putting me off my meal.'

Afterwards we moved back through to the lounge with a pot of coffee. Fitzroy indicated we should sit in the chairs by the fire. He brought the notes we had been working on across but placed them on the small table.

'Summarise,' he said.

'Of the people I know personally, particularly of the ones who observed me in the antechamber, I believe only Hans has the stamina to have slipped away, killed Richard, and rejoined the others without being missed. Looking at the map and from my memory I traced the shortest discreet path and I do not believe Richenda could run that far without becoming obviously red in the face and sweating from exertion. I would have included Merry too, but if she is pregnant it seems less likely. Bertram certainly could not have managed it. So, while those four all had a degree of motive, some more than others, only Hans could have managed it successfully – I believe.'

'I agree,' said Fitzroy, sipping his coffee. 'What are Hans' motives?'

'His potential motives include the way Richard has treated his wife, if he did actually expect to inherit Stapleford Hall when Richenda gave birth – as the will indicated - and he mentioned when he came to speak to me that he had had difficult business dealings with Richard. I remember, before we went north for the New Year to Richard's castle, it was discussed between us that he needed to acquire more business. His German name was already beginning to affect his success. Richard offered to help.'

Fitzroy nodded. 'And he asked you to run away with him. Do you believe that was an attempt to divert attention from himself and stall the case?'

I gazed into the fire. I did not trust myself to face him. 'Not entirely. Before he married, Hans made it clear on more than one occasion that he would have preferred to marry me over Richenda if he had not been in need of a bride with a dowry.'

'Good God, girl. Will you stop making these stupid men fall for you!'

'I have actually thought about this and I do not believe it is my fault.'

Fitzroy tapped me on the arm, so I had to face him. 'This I have to hear.'

'In general, the men who have "fallen" for me have been with me in a number of difficult situations when emotions, often fear for their lives, is heightened...'

'And you survived. I will allow that would affect their judgement.'

'Also,' I said carefully, 'I have frequently been the only attractive young woman present and I believe I am unusually articulate.'

Fitzroy shrugged. 'At least you are aware of why these things happen. Do not, for heaven's sake, go putting the cat among the pigeons in the service and setting agent against agent as they vie for your affections.' He shivered. 'It doesn't bear thinking about.'

I assumed he was joking but didn't press it. 'I do believe, regardless of his intentions, that Hans looks on me with fondness. His marriage to Richenda has its difficulties, and we are aware that he has a preference for small dark-haired mistresses rather than more… professional women.'

'He doesn't use prostitutes,' said Fitzroy. 'I understand that, but why did he think you would run away with him? Are you more involved with him than I have realised?'

I clenched my coffee cup tightly. 'Bertram is without question the love of my life, even if he no longer feels the same way. I will allow that Hans Muller is attractive, but I have no desire to be his mistress – or even if it had been possible, his wife.'

'Do you think he is our killer?'

'I think it is possible, but there is no hard evidence.'

'Do you think he did it?'

'I think it would be unlike him to stab someone. He prides himself on being even-tempered and diplomatic. He is charming and I have never felt that he is concealing a hot temper.'

'No, he's more coldly determined to get his way. He allows logic to rule him,' said Fitzroy. 'I actually don't mind him. But you're right, I cannot see him stabbing Richard in a fit of passion, and in such a way that drew an enormous an amount of attention.'

'I agree. He would plan a murder carefully,' I said. 'So, you believe the stabbing was an impulsive act?'

Fitzroy nodded. 'They usually are. And rarely by women – though some, such as yourself, would not be beyond stabbing someone if they deserved it. That's a compliment, by the way.'

'Thank you,' I said. 'In summary, Hans could have done it, but it is very unlikely that he did.'

Fitzroy nodded again. 'Always useful to have a back-up culprit who's believable if you need to get the real culprit off.'

'Are we trying to do that?' I asked.

'Not this time. We agree this is an impulsive, unplanned crime by someone who had a serious grudge against Richard...'

'Someone who perhaps had no other opportunity to get close to him...'

'Because they were a servant, or were normally living some distance from him,' finished Fitzroy for me. 'Your mother could have done it. She has a coiled viper of anger inside her. Fortunately, her bishop appears to be able to keep her in line.'

'You're suggesting my mother...'

'No,' said Fitzroy, 'I'm giving an example of the personality type who might have done this. Someone who had suffered for a long time at Richard's hand and...'

'Snapped,' I said.

'Exactly,' said Fitzroy. 'We, at the very least, have an idea of the sort of person who committed this crime.'

'And we also know it is someone Richard was either once fond of – if that's possible -'

'Or he didn't regard as being very important,' said Fitzroy.

'Because he would rather I took the blame.'

'You must have got deeply under his skin,' said spy with a smile. 'Well done. Useful skill.'

'I didn't do it deliberately.'

Fitzroy shrugged. 'Oh well, you can always reflect on how you did it later and learn from it.'

Or how you do it, I thought silently.

'What conclusion did you come to with the guests?'

'It is likely the absence of someone from the front pews would have been noticed. None of the witness statements mention this. Neither was anyone observed with blood on their clothing.'

'That is a point that is bothering me,' said Fitzroy. 'But continue.'

'Then it starts getting more difficult. Everyone present knew one or two people other than Bertram, myself, and our families, but most of them did not know each other. There also seems to have been some confusion with the ushers and the seating, so that people were milling around.'

'Good, you noticed that. Only three people referred to that – and then obliquely.'

'You think it might have been orchestrated?' I asked.

'It's hard to see how it might have been done if this was an impulsive act, but I may be missing something. Wedding etiquette is not my forte. You've discounted Joe, of course?'

'My brother?' An icy wave slid down my spine.

'Don't worry. He is neither strong enough or tall enough to have inflicted the damage. Although I bet he could have run fast and unnoticed, if he wanted to. Plus, if he had any idea how Richard treated you, he might have decided to stab him on impulse. I doubt he would have been motivated by more than anger – certainly, he wouldn't have thought of the consequences. Don't look so worried. I told you he didn't do it.'

I let out the breath I hadn't realised I had been holding. 'It does require a lack of emotion, this work.'

'I did tell you. Everything and everyone must be considered in matters of intelligence, despite one's personal bias. But it's been a long day, let me cut matters short. Neither of us have alighted on any one person in particular who wished Richard desperately ill. Many of the guests may have disliked him – and indeed we both identified several we know did – but I suspect that whatever drove someone to this desperate act was not only a recent turn of events, but something they were desperate to keep silent.'

'You mean they were in some way complicit?' I said.

'Possibly. Generally respectable people, like those at your wedding, will go to the police with a grievance. If they haven't...'

'There has to be a reason,' I finished. 'But could it not be that they thought they would not be believed over a powerful and influential man like Richard?'

'Also possible,' said Fitzroy. 'Here,' he handed me over a piece of paper. On it he had written

Culprit

Desperate

Reasonably strong

At least five foot five by angle of entry

Impulsive, passionate crime

Culprit's motive is either incriminating or has to be kept secret

Does Culprit usually have no access to Richard – due to station or location

Must be able to move quickly to not be spotted

Why were they not observed to have blood on their clothing?

Culprit considered unimportant by Richard who would rather blame Euphemia

Unlikely to have been direct family, unless observed leaving the pews

He had scribbled at the bottom, *Problem with ushering? Caused by culprit?*

'When did you write this?' I asked.

'Just before I came to see you,' said Fitzroy. 'After I'd had a quick squint at the corpse.'

'I expect it took you – what, half an hour? To formulate

45

this?'

'More like ten minutes,' said Fitzroy. 'I've been doing this a long time.'

'But we spent all day…'

'This is the boring bit about intelligence work,' said Fitzroy. 'I might have been able to think of this in the moment, but I needed to verify my thoughts. That is what today was about.'

'I think I see,' I said. 'It's very frustrating. Of course, we are assuming everyone is telling the truth and that no one is concealing matters for the sake of another.'

'Ugh, don't. If we had found something of note we would have re-interviewed the subject. I did cross-reference what was said, didn't you? And I found no inconsistencies. The last thing we need is some kind of conspiracy,' said Fitzroy. 'Fortunately, I thought of that before we started, so we don't have to go over it all again. A person's word is generally worth less than the air used to form it.'

'Do you mean don't trust anyone?'

'I am not going to dignify that with an answer. You will note we learned one detail: that your ushers were not particularly competent.'

'We should check one of them did not slip away,' I said.

'Good thought,' said Fitzroy. 'Now, Alice, if I were you, I'd head to bed. We're leaving early in the morning.'

'We're leaving? To go where?'

Fitzroy flashed me a smile. 'That's need to know – and you don't.'

I went upstairs smothering down the feeling of wanting to shake him until his teeth rattled. Not, I thought, that I would be able to, but it seemed to me only one of us was enjoying my initiation and it was not I.

Chapter Five

The next morning, we were up and away before dawn. Fitzroy had lent me an extra coat to put over my own. He'd also wound a scarf tightly round my neck. 'It will be freezing until the sun is up.' I yawned and wished the coffee pot had not emptied so quickly.

'How will you be able to see?' I asked.

'Oh, I know the road. As long as the other chaps have their lamps lit, we'll be fine.'

I clambered into the car too sleepy to be afraid. This changed after less than half an hour. Despite the extra layers I could feel the cold seeping into my bones. Also, Fitzroy drove with his usual speed. I had been tired after our labours yesterday and thought I had slept well, but I was wracked by yawns. The spy had gone to his room, how long after me I did not know, but he showed no signs of fatigue.

'Are you not tired?' I enquired, trying to be tactful.

'I got at least four hours last night. I should be fine,' he said, turning briefly to smile at me. 'Don't worry, I'm not expecting an in-depth dissection of our conversation yesterday. I need to concentrate until the sun comes up. You can snooze if you want.'

'I would very much like to, but I am too cold.'

'There's coffee in the back for later. For now, I want to make good time. After I've dropped you off, I still have a long drive.'

This did waken me. 'You're leaving me?'

'Indeed,' said the spy. 'Your first solo engagement. It's so easy it's hardly a mission. Just re-interviewing some people about what happened at your wedding. Hardly work at all.'

'Who?'

'You'll see.'

'And I can't tell them I'm working for the Crown?'

'Absolutely not. You can't say you are an asset, an agent, or even helping the police. It's imperative that you don't say anything of the kind to any of the people you will meet. Do you understand, Alice?'

'Yes, I will take care.'

'You cannot take it on yourself to tell them any of this any under any circumstance. That is an order. Breaking it will have serious consequences.'

'I understand. Am I going undercover? Are they expecting me?'

'Oh, yes, they are expecting you, but simply as Euphemia. As I said it's an easy task.'

'When will you pick me up again?'

'I'll let you know. Probably a couple of days if all goes well.'

'You're not telling me where you are going, are you?'

'No, Alice, I'm not. But, believe it or not, I do have some things on my plate that don't relate directly to you.'

I licked my lips and instantly regretted it as I felt them beginning to chap. Normally, I would have said exactly what I was thinking. Now I had to use more tact. One of the aspects of my relationship with Fitzroy that I had cherished - realistically the only one I had cherished - had been the ability to say anything I liked to him in any manner. This privilege had been removed.

'You're thinking that I said we'd have forty-eight hours to investigate your situation, aren't you?'

'Yes!'

'Don't look so surprised. We know each other better than you realise. That aside, I am giving you more than a couple of days to investigate. When I return, I will do my best to spare more time. I appreciate that you need the shadow of suspicion lifted from your name - and I intend on doing my damn best to help you. However, that is not my job, and I do have to do my job.'

'I know,' I said. 'The work comes first.'

'Always, Alice. Even with you.'

Conversation between us halted as we came to some extremely twisty bits of the road. Fitzroy skidded on one corner but recovered the car smoothly enough. The only damage was to my heart, which beat so fast I thought my clothes must be vibrating. The spy briefly touched my hand, as if to say everything was fine, before he threw us into another series of seemingly life-threatening corners. I stole a look at his face. He had a look of intense concentration, unlike the casual fearlessness he had displayed on our previous journey. Wherever he was taking me, it was clear he didn't actually have time for it. He was doing his best for me and I knew I should be more grateful. I decided that sitting on the edge of my seat, so obviously scared he had to reassure me, was not helpful. With a determined effort, I slid back in my seat and closed my eyes. The first few seconds were the worst as I felt more strongly than ever the car skittered underneath me. But I kept my eyes shut and miraculously, despite the cold, I fell asleep.

When I awoke dawn had broken and the pale, grey light of the early day revealed the landscape around us. 'But, I know this place!' I said, sitting up. 'This is near the Muller estate.

'Exactly,' said Fitzroy, 'I'm taking you home - or as near to it as I can get you.'

'I've failed?' I asked abashed.

'Don't be melodramatic, Alice. You can't fail once you're in the service, you're in for life. I can't take you where I am going, and this is an excellent opportunity for you to look over your home ground with fresh eyes. You may not realise this, but even the people who are closest to you often hold secrets. For example, there is a significant chance that Merry is Mrs Wilson's child.'

'What? That's impossible. She said her family were in London.'

'She told you were she grew up and who she believed to be her parents. Have you never wondered why she was taken into the household so young? She told you that herself. And you told me she was treated as something of a family pet. The Stapleford family were never known for their charitable attitude - despite Richenda's attempts to help streetwalkers - why would they take in and care for such a young maid?'

'Good God! Are you sure?'

'No, but taking all the factors into account, it is a strong possibility.'

'Does she know?'

'It's never been of relevance before.'

'You mean, despite being pregnant, she might have had a strong enough reason to…'

'The affair was with Richard's father, not Richard,' said Fitzroy. 'But it doesn't mean complications might not have arisen. You always suspected he killed his illegitimate sister in the asylum.'

'I thought she was Mrs Wilson's only daughter!'

'In the normal way of things women are capable of bearing more than one child, Alice.'

I sat dumbfounded. Part of me wondered if this was some

kind of test. He had suggested a hypothesis without offering evidence. If it were true, it might provide Merry with a motive for murder. Especially if she thought Richard might harm her, or her unborn child. Nausea swept over me. Of all the people in the world I didn't want the murderer to be, Merry was second, right after my brother Joe.

'All right if I drop you by the gates?' said Fitzroy. 'The chap should be awake and can take you up the drive in a dog cart. I need to get away.'

'Of course,' I said. 'Good luck.' I managed to jump lightly out, so he didn't have to stop the car to come and help me.

Fitzroy smiled. 'I've put some reading material in your bag. Stuff on the role of the monarchy vis-à-vis the role of parliament and some basic police law. Nothing secret, but you need to know how things work.'

'In my bag? But it was under my bed. How did...'

The spy touched his finger to his nose and winked at me. Then, giving me a salute, he turned the car and drove away. I picked up my bag, which did indeed feel heavier, and went to knock on the gatehouse door.

Chiltern, the gatekeeper, appeared more dismayed to have to leave his breakfast than surprised to see me. His wife put it in the oven and told him sternly to take me up to the big house. It might have been nothing but my own fancy, but I rather thought before the murder she might have asked if I would like something myself, for my stomach was growling loudly. But then, I had never known the Chilterns more than to nod at them when I went past. They had always been a solitary couple on an estate that was becoming known for its community.

Chiltern delivered me to the door, placed my bag at my feet, and was back in his cart before I had even rung the bell.

The door opened and the familiar face of Stone gazed impassively at me. 'Welcome home, miss,' he said. 'May I take your bag? The family are eating breakfast. Would you care to join them, or would you like to go up to your room first?'

'I think I should straighten up before joining them,' I said. 'Perhaps you would be so kind as to let them know I am here? Maybe in about ten minutes.'

'As you wish, miss,' said Stone.

'I take Mr Bertram is still in residence?'

'Indeed, Mr Stapleford and your mother have remained with us.'

Wonderful, I thought. My mother would have plenty to say to me. Stone must have noticed my expression. As he left me outside my room, he said, 'Might I suggest I apprise the family in twenty minutes to half an hour.'

'But they will want to know who rang the bell,' I said.

'Ah,' said Stone. 'I do believe that I hear someone calling me from the kitchen. The new boot-boy has doubtless caused an upset again. He is remarkably clumsy. When he last broke one of Cook's serving dishes, it took me quite some time to calm her down.'

'About twenty minutes to half an hour?' I said with a slight smile.

'Exactly, miss.'

I watched him walk away and wondered why Fitzroy had never thought of engaging a butler to work as an agent of the Crown. They appeared to have all the right qualities. I opened the door and walked softly into my room.

It had been cleaned since the wedding, but there were still some signs of my wedding preparations. Extra blooms that I had not used in my bouquet - all the flowers having come from the gardens here - stood neatly trimmed in a tall vase.

My suitcase, with my honeymoon clothes, sat in the centre of my made bed.

I unpacked my small bag, leaving dirty clothes for the maid to wash and restocking it with other suitable garments. I did indeed find several rather dryly titled books. I sat them on my night stand. I had the impression from the spy it was more important for me to read these than it was for me to ensure I brought them with me when he fetched me. At the bottom I also found a small tool I did not immediately recognise. It took me a few minutes to figure out it was a button hook.[8] I added only one evening dress to the bag. I doubted I would need it, but I imagined I was meant to be prepared for anything. I had the bag redone and ready to go quickly. I slid it under my bed. That I was about to disappear again was a conversation I did not wish to have as an opener. Besides, I did not know how long it would be before Fitzroy returned.

It appeared my ewer had been filled as usual. I took off my hat and washed off the grime from the road. On the spur of the moment I decided to change into a fresh dress, more like the ones I would have worn at home. I found the buttonhook remarkably easy to use and very helpful. I appreciated Fitzroy's practicality.

With impeccable timing I saw Stone entering the breakfast room as I came down the final stairs. I had set one foot on the polished hallway floor when I heard a roar from the room ahead. Bertram charged through the breakfast room doors. He skidded to a halt when he saw me. I smiled and reached out my hands to him. He did not approach.

'Where is he?' he roared. 'Where is the bounder?'

---

[8]No respectable lady ever owns a button hook, as she had a maid to tend to her. Most often it is ladies of the night who use such things.

I started back, tripping over the bottom step and sitting down hard.

'Where is who?

Bertram stalked over towards me, like a slightly portly tiger, and stopped a couple of feet in front of me. He did not offer a hand to help me up. Inside he gazed down at me, his eyes blazing. 'The man you ran away with! That cad, Fitzroy, who else?'

Chapter Six

I stared back at him open-mouthed. This, I realised, must be part of my training. I had to explain to my furious fiancé that I had not run off with a spy but had left with him for some reason that did not relate to his work as an agent of the Crown. I tried to think of an explanation, but nothing came. All I could think of was how much I wanted to slap Fitzroy at that moment.

'Euphemia!' Richenda ran across the hall as fast as her diet of cake would allow. She reached down and pulled me up and into a smothering embrace. 'I am so glad you are safe,' she said. 'I never thought those terrible rumours could be true.' I surfaced with some difficulty. With more skill than I would have imagined, Richenda kept herself between me and Bertram as she guided me back towards the breakfast room.

'Which rumours?' I asked softly. I had seen Richenda's face in the anteroom, and I had seen she thought I had killed Richard. However, I had also seen her decide within seconds to stand by her friend and protect me as much as she was able. I could feel tears pricking the back of my eyes. Despite everything - despite the fact her husband flirted with me and she thought I might have killed her twin - she seemed genuinely delighted to see me.

'Nothing. Nothing. All nonsense,' said Richenda, her arm possessively around my shoulders. 'Your mother is still here. She will be overjoyed to see you.' I doubted that, but with Bertram circling us like prey I felt my best chance of sorting this encounter was among others.

We entered the breakfast room. Hans, who had been seated at the top of the table, stood and came forward at once. He took both my hands, even though I had not held them out to him. 'I am delighted you are home,' he said, staring intently down at me. 'Truly I am.' And he gave my hands an urgent squeeze. Looking into his eyes I saw the desperate hope that I would not mention to Richenda that he had offered to spirit me away to thwart justice and have me become his mistress.

'Joe, go to your room,' said my mother's voice.

'But it's Effie. Effie's come back!' He escaped my mother's lunge by diving under the table and crawling out towards me. He pushed Hans aside and hugged me. Hans stood back smiling benevolently. He moved to place both a restraining, and at the same time supportive, hand on my mother's shoulder. He gave a small chuckle. 'It seems I am not the only one overjoyed to see Euphemia returned to the bosom of her family.' He threw a look at Bertram as if reminding him to behave himself in another man's house. Or, at least, that is how I would have read the situation before. Now, I saw beneath Hans's charm and realised his desperate, manipulative attempts to lighten the atmosphere in the room and keep the truth from his wife. All the time he kept trying to catch my eyes, trying to predict what I might do. I wondered how many times before he had deceived us. It was all so well done. I could not help remembering what Fitzroy had said about those closest to us concealing secrets. I still had no plan.

I hugged Joe with real affection. 'I am so pleased to see you again, Joe,' I said.

He leant back to look up at me. One day he would be much taller than I, but for now he was simply a little boy gazing up at his big sister. 'Everything will be alright now,

Effie,' he said. 'You're home and we will all take care of you.' He gave me a tighter squeeze and I burst into tears.

I felt overwrought, so the tears came easily. At the same time, I knew an outward sign of my distress would display more quickly what the true feelings of the others were to me.

My mother broke away from Hans. 'Here. Here,' she said, fluttering her hands about. 'Let her go, Joe. You'll hurt her. You don't know your own strength.' She removed Joe with a mother's dexterity and led me over to a chair. 'My poor girl is overwrought. Can someone please fetch a brandy and some smelling salts?'

'She's overwrought,' said Bertram. 'Euphemia's overwrought. Oh well then. We must all take care of her. No matter that she disappeared two days ago without a care for anyone else. It's not like her fiancé had a heart condition or anything, is it? It's not like the man who had been about to pledge his love and life to her in front of all his friends might be a little concerned at her vanishing. It's not like his elder brother just died. Oh no, let's all comfort Euphemia!'

I looked up at him. My breath laboured, and within my ribcage I could feel a crushing pain. 'But you mentioned Fitzroy. You knew where I was.'

'You admit it? Good God!' said Bertram. 'You were somewhere with Fitzroy. Well, that makes it all fine and dandy, doesn't it!'

Richenda gave him an odd look. 'He is a policeman, Bertram. I do not believe he would be involved in any kind of improper behaviour.'

Bertram grew red in the face. His breath built up inside him, but all that he said was a very loud 'Bah!' Before he stormed out. As an asset, he was unable to say what Fitzroy was and also that the spy frequently engaged in the most improper behaviour. Richenda knew him only as the kind man who had arranged the rescue of her children on a previous occasion.

'I presume you had to testify about your innocence or some such thing?' said my mother.

I nodded. Fitzroy was right. I was a terrible liar and the less I said the better it would be. Laughter bubbled inside me, but I pushed it down as I realised that the only explanation I would need would be the one my family had concocted themselves. With the exception of Bertram's version of course. I hated my situation. I hated the fact that they had been upset, but I now understood why Fitzroy often said so little. Their own assumptions would be much more powerful than any story I might conceive of.

'And, of course, you had a police chaperon with you,' said Hans. His tone suggested a statement, but I could see a question in his eyes. After all, I had not immediately refused his offer nor taken serious offence. In fact, I appeared to have picked up his implied idea of my becoming his mistress remarkably quickly. He thought of me as a sheltered young woman, whereas the reality of working on the Crown's business had opened my eyes to many aspects of life that he would not have dreamed I knew. Mistresses were a mere peccadillo of gentlemen compared to the sleazy businesses of brothels.[9] From my perspective he had been all too explicit, and I had been too shocked to find the words to answer him. That he would willingly deceive Richenda was one thing; after all, his previous mistresses had been between his marriages. But that he would think I would agree to such a thing? That he would actually ask… No, Hans had sunk a great deal in my opinion.

Richenda's voice drew me from my thoughts. 'My

---

[9] I had once almost accidentally joined one…

brother does tend to verge on the melodramatic. Although, of course, it was a trying day for both of us. But I have quite got over it.' I saw her chin tremble as she said this. 'Bertram should be thanking his lucky stars that Euphemia is returned safe to us.'

'Well said, my wife,' said Hans. I turned my head to throw him as disgusted a look as I dared. I swear he flinched slightly. Whatever I said, I was now certain Hans would back me up on anything that did not include the true version of events and his part in them.

Richenda blushed under her husband's praise. They had not been seated close together, but perhaps out of this dreadful incident would come some good and they would reforge their marriage.

'Joe, why don't you go and fetch Mr Stapleford,' said my mother.

Joe nodded eagerly and ran off.

'He will hardly refuse the boy,' said my mother. 'I suggest when he returns we all make ourselves scarce so my daughter and Bertram can speak.' She patted me awkwardly on the shoulder. 'While you are speaking with him, I will get Glanville to draw you a bath and then you can rest. You must be exhausted after your ordeal.'

'Thank you, Mama,' I said obediently. 'If it is not too much trouble, I would quite like some breakfast. I have been travelling since early this morning and have yet to eat.' I regretted the words as soon as they were out of my mouth, because, of course, everyone then began clambering to know where I had come from. They were all speaking at once, but how I was to deal with them without pretending to faint was beyond me. I did not fancy falling off my chair here as I knew the carpet to be particularly thin.

However, all conversation stopped when Bertram

appeared in the doorway. Joe stood slightly behind him, for all the world like a guard dog determined not to let his sheep escape the field. 'I'll get the kitchen to send you up some fresh stuff,' said Richenda and brushed past Bertram. I suppressed a smile. I knew all too well she would take this opportunity to order a separate tray for herself to replace the repast she had to leave behind.

'If you have no objection, Mr Muller, I will visit your guest,' said my mother. 'An older woman's counsel will be helpful. Joe will go to the library and do his Latin.' Joe's face was a picture of outraged innocence, but he had hardly time to draw breath before my mother was hustling him out. Hans left last. He gave Bertram a manly clap on the shoulder, but his expression as he passed me was both wary and worried. He shut the door behind him.

'Did Rory not tell you where I had been taken?' I said, forestalling Bertram. I knew full well Rory McLeod had no idea where I had gone, but I needed to know what he had said. A small part of me wished Fitzroy was here to see how I was doing. The larger part of myself hated that I would have to lie to Bertram and wanted to put that moment off as long as possible.

Bertram's jaw dropped and his mouth formed a perfect O. I had not previously noticed the pleasing symmetry of his face. He put a hand down on the table and made contact with an egg plate. He lowered himself into a seat. I passed him a napkin and he began to wipe his hand.

'Did he?' I persisted.

'Rory? My Rory McLeod was here? But we decided not to invite him to the wedding.' Bertram's anger appeared to have been swallowed by his confusion. He continued to wipe his now clean hand.

'He was the police official summoned by the local

constabulary. They did not have anyone of sufficient seniority to conduct the enquiry. I thought he would have questioned you along with the other witnesses?'

Bertram shook his head. 'I only saw ordinary bobbies taking statements. McLeod? Are you sure? You haven't suffered a concussion, have you?'

I smiled at him. 'No, not at all. Apparently, after leaving you, he approached Fitzroy for a position and I presume that he, in turn, opened the way for Rory into the police force. He is a methodical man, and working with us, perhaps he acquired the desire to see justice done more in our world.'

'Well, if he wanted to do that, he certainly wouldn't have wanted to work with *that man*. He didn't hurt you, did he?'

'Rory? No. He wasn't exactly kind, and he made it perfectly clear he thought me capable of killing. He has quite a low opinion of me.'

'Does he, by Jove,' said Bertram, the colour coming back into his cheeks. It cheered me to see him firing up in my defence. 'But no, I didn't mean him. McLeod wouldn't hurt a fly. I meant the other one.'

'Fitzroy?' I said astonished. 'He would never hurt me - or any female. He has a great regard for my sex.'

Bertram made a harrumphing noise.

'So, what were you told about my absence? It had not occurred to me you would be left in the dark.' In fact, it had not occurred to me at all to think of the people I had left behind. I decided to blame this on shock.

'The local sergeant said you had been officially released without charge and that you had been taken away by an official to finalise matters. He couldn't give me the man's name, but he described him.'

'So that's how you knew Fitzroy was here.'

'He gets damn everywhere,' said Bertram. 'I thought we

had agreed to remove him from our lives.'

I changed the direction of the conversation. 'I hope you do now believe I am innocent.'

'Yes, well. It was all a bit of surprise opening the door and seeing you covered in blood. At first, I thought you were hurt, didn't take in the fact that there was a body at your feet until Merry nudged me.'

'She noticed first?' I said.

'No idea. Can't speak for the others, but I was floored. I mean... no one in the right mind would say my brother was a good man. I imagine most folk disliked him. A few of us knew how damn well evil he was. We know he killed our father. Maybe more. Wouldn't have blamed you if you'd offed him in self-defence. I know he'd treated you badly too, I just didn't know how badly. The scene made me wonder if it was worse than you'd told me. If you'd snapped. But whatever it was, you should have come to me, Euphemia. To me. Not tried to deal with it on your own. I thought we were partners in all things. I thought you trusted me.'

At this I stood up and went to kneel at his feet. I took one of his hands in mine. He tried to tug me to get up, but I resisted. 'Oh, my darling, I would trust you with my very soul. I found Richard dying. He wanted to me to pull out the knife and when I did, his blood...' I faltered as I remembered the moment. 'His blood...' I got no further as Bertram stood and pulled me into his arms. He kissed me passionately. I responded with equal pleasure and relief. Being in his arms felt like coming home. When he parted his lips from mine, I laid my head on his shoulder and closed my eyes. If only everything could go back to what it was. My poor love had no idea that a shadow now stood between us, and I would have to lie to him for a while longer. Would I ever tell him the truth? Would he ever forgive my choice if I did?

I was so wrapped up in my own thoughts that I barely realised Bertram was speaking. 'So, a small ceremony then. It will have to be after the funeral, but I thought…'

I raised my head. 'Bertram, I cannot possibly marry you until I have cleared my name.'

Bertram released me and took a step back. 'No, Euphemia. Leave this to the police. Don't get involved.' He took a deep breath. 'It's that bloody man, isn't it? He's convinced you you have to find my brother's killer. Well, I don't want you to. He was a twisted, evil cad and I am glad he's dead. Just let it lie. I beg you.'

Tears that had clung to my eyelashes broke free as I shook my head. 'I can't.'

Bertram raised his fists to the ceiling. 'That bloody man. Will he never leave us alone!'

Our conversation finished where we had started, with Bertram storming out of the room.

Chapter Seven

Bertram absented himself from dinner that night. Richenda and Hans sat at opposite ends of the table. My mother sat on one side. Little Joe had been banished to the nursery to eat. I could imagine his disgust.

'Did the Bishop not remain?' I asked my mother as we began our soup.

'He wanted to, of course,' said my mother, 'but ecclesiastical business pressed. I, however, had no intention of leaving until my daughter was located, and so I told him.'

'I am sure he understood,' said Richenda.

My mother sniffed ever so slightly. 'I have a great regard for my husband, but I do not allow him to control my actions.' She tried the soup. 'Very nice, Richenda, a good beefy stock. Your cook has let the bones caramelise properly. But, yes, the Bishop had expected me to stay. Indeed, I believe he would have done so too, if he could. Dear man.'

Richenda frowned as she worked her way through the labyrinth of my mother's speech.

'I am so very sorry you did not know I was safe,' I said carefully. 'It never occurred to me that you would not be given full details.'

'It was Bertram who went up to the police station,' said Richenda. 'When we heard nothing from you the following morning, he telephoned the station and was told you had been released, but no more. He got himself into quite a state.'

'No one could persuade him not to go up there himself

and demand answers,' said my mother.

'He made himself ill,' said Hans.

'Oh no,' I said.

'He is quite well now,' interrupted my mother. 'It was merely a small turn.' She shot Hans a gimlet look. Hans caught my eye.

'Indeed, he was fortunate. We must hope nothing occurs to disturb him further.'

In my mind's eye I imagined sticking my fork in Hans' hand. He still feared I would reveal his uncouth offer. I would have to speak to him.

'Who now heads the investigation?' I asked.

'Oh, it's all solved,' said Richenda. 'It turns out that when they looked into it, the police found there had been several sightings of a tramp in the countryside. They assume he had come into the church for warmth, or maybe he intended to rob the poor box. Only Richard found him. Well, you know my twin, he would not have dealt kindly with the man.'

'It is unfortunate he had a knife,' said my mother. 'Or the worst sustained would have been bruises on both sides.' She took a good swallow of wine. 'I abhor man's innate tendency to violence.'

'As do we all, Mama,' I said. 'But where did this tramp find the knife?'

'Oh, it came from our kitchen,' said Richenda easily. 'Cook had the windows open with all the baking she was doing. The police believe he must have reached through one and lifted it.'

'To be clear,' broke in Hans, 'they do not believe the man intended to murder my brother-in-law, but that he took the knife to facilitate an easier life for himself. For the cutting of wood and such things.'

It was on the tip of my tongue to ask where the knife was now. I could not recall it clearly. 'How extraordinary,' I said. 'How fate and fortune intertwines.'

My mother nodded. 'You should talk to your step-father about that. He has many interesting things to say on the matter of luck and misfortune.'

'Perhaps we should turn to happier topics,' suggested Hans. The dinner continued in a slightly awkward manner, but I had no doubt that at least my mother and Richenda welcomed my return.

After dinner we all retired early to our rooms. I believe we all sought the normality of routine as much as we sought not to indulge in further conversation. I did not believe the story of the tramp for one moment and I doubted the others did either. However, there appeared to be an unspoken acceptance of the ridiculous idea. I mourned Richard no more than the others, but the easy lie of his death troubled me. I decided to take a turn about the gardens before I settled for the night. My mind raced with thoughts and I knew I would only toss and turn if I went to bed.

The moon shone three-quarters full gilding the gardens with silver. The scent of jasmine hung heavy on the air and somewhere an owl hooted. The night had turned unusually mild. As I paced, I grew gradually calmer. I shuffled the information I had gained in my mind. I had an itch at the back of my brain. I knew I had heard something important. At that moment, Hans appeared around the edge of a hedge. I started and jumped back. I kept enough of my awareness not to scream. 'Whatever are you doing?' I asked.

'I might as ask you the same, sister? Did you not hear at dinner that there is a tramp on the loose who has killed?'

'I am not your sister...'

'But you and Bertram have made up, have you not? And

66

you will be?'

'Can I help you with something, Hans?'

'I spotted you from my study and I was concerned for your safety.'

'I have found this walled estate to be most safe during my time here,' I said. 'I assume if this tramp remains unapprehended you have put further measures in place. You take such good care of the people in your charge.'

'Take my arm, Euphemia, and we can walk together. Like old times.'

'I would rather not,' I said, keeping my distance.

'You cannot think that I would harm you in any way?' said Hans, sounding genuinely shocked.

'No, I do not think that,' I said. 'But I do think our last conversation – before my departure – has left a mark upon our friendship that will take some time to fade.'

'I wanted to save you from the noose. I could not bear to think of... I was open and honest with you.'

'As you are not with your wife.'

'Have you told her?'

'No, and if it eases your mind, I have every intention of forgetting the words we exchanged that night.'

'You did not refuse me, Euphemia.'

'Hans, leave it be. I will marry Bertram in time, and we will forget all this.'

'Speaking of Bertram, I see the very man closing upon us. I will leave you together.' As Hans walked away, I recalled what Fitzroy had said; if Hans had murdered Richard then secretly helping me flee would turn suspicion away from him. I felt sick to my stomach. Hans did not strike me as a killer - but an impulsive action on the back of a threat from Richard?

'You look very sombre,' said Bertram. 'Was that Hans,

walking with you?'

'I heard at dinner that you had been unwell.'

'Shouldn't have tried to strangle the on-duty bobby with his own collar.'

'You are joking, aren't you?'

Bertram dropped his head slightly in a sheepish manner. 'I was rather upset about the whole thing.'

I put my arms round his neck and kissed him lightly on the lips. 'I would very much prefer it if you did not allow your temper to finish you off before we can marry.'

'Me too,' said Bertram. 'It is all a terrible mess. I don't believe the tramp rubbish, do you?'

'No, I think something came out of Richard's past and killed him.'

'Evil deeds catching up and all that?'

I nodded. 'To be honest, my love, if I was not under suspicion – and I will always be under suspicion until the killer is caught – I probably would not trouble much, even if he was your brother.'

Bertram slipped my hand through his arm and began to walk again. 'Better not to stay still. We might be overheard,' he said. 'No, I wouldn't bother much either. Seems a terrible thing to say of one's own kin, but he was never lovable, even as a child. I hadn't thought much about you being under a cloud for this…'

'Stain on my reputation,' I said wryly. 'You cannot make me believe that people are not talking about this the length and breadth of the county – if not further abroad. It is not as if they have caught an actual tramp, is it?'

'No. I used the same sort of nonsense back when Papa was killed. Fortunately, no one ever suspected me.'

I patted his arm. 'You are not a killer.'

'Thank you,' said Bertram. 'I have always hoped my

future bride would feel that way.'

I laughed. 'Where are we going?'

'Why, over to the church,' said Bertram. 'You want to take another look at the scene, don't you?'

'I would not have asked you to come with me.'

'Well, I dashed well am not going to have you wandering around a creepy old church looking for a murderer without me. What kind of man do you think I am?'

'A brave, faithful, and loyal one,' I said.

'You make me sound like a dog,' said Bertram.

'But not a sheep,' I said.

'What?'

'Old joke. Never mind. I appreciate your concern and would be most happy to accept your offer of assistance.'

'What are we looking for?' asked Bertram.

'I really have no idea.'

'Oh good, same as usual then.'

We walked in companionable silence until we came to the church. 'Oh, will it be…' Bertram produced a key. 'I know how you think,' he said. 'Where do we start.'

'I confess I am not keen to re-enter the antechamber, but that is where our most serious search must be done. Perhaps we could start with a general sweep of the church?' Bertram assented. 'We should also check the pathways around the church in case -' I broke off.

'In case anyone whoever killed him went out the back.'

'I do not consider it could be you,' I said.

'Then you are a better person than I,' said Bertram. 'I did genuinely wonder if you had killed Richard. I wouldn't have blamed you…'

I stopped and laid both hands on his arm. 'I know I can be both passionate and headstrong,' I said, 'but I promise you I would never take a life in such a state. I know myself. My anger leads to no more violence than the occasional slap.'

'I hope the one you gave Fitzroy last time was a good one.'

'It had a ring to it,' I said. 'The skin on his face flamed.'

'It's a wonder you got it past him to be honest,' said Bertram, prising his arm free to unlock the church door.

'He let me hit him,' I said.

'You're not going to try and convince me that man felt remorse, are you?' said Bertram pushing the door open. 'Because I don't believe it.'

'I have no way of knowing what goes on in his head,' I said. 'But I agree, I would not be able to get one past him in general.'

Bertram pecked me on the cheek. 'Well, I am damn glad you did. If my ticker wasn't so dodgy, I'd have given that man a thrashing a dozen times over.' These words were spoken with an edge that surprised me. I knew Bertram disliked the spy, but this sounded as if he hated him. I let the topic go for now and appealed to his chivalrous instinct. I caught at his arm again.

'Gosh,' I said, 'it does look much bigger and more foreboding in the darkness.'

Bertram produced a lighter from his pocket. 'I'll get those candles lit in a trice. You'll see there is nothing to be afraid of. I'll say this for Hans, he does have a lovely little church.' He wandered off dotting lights across the main body of the church. I followed him. Having grown up a vicar's daughter I have no fear of churches, the deceased, or even corpses, but better to let Bertram think he was in charge. Even as I thought this I gasped inwardly. Was I merely playing the clever fiancée who did not want her beau to feel bad – manipulating him as women have done to their men down the centuries – or was I taking on more and more of the attitudes of a spy.

'Hey, Euphemia!'

I turned around to see Bertram standing in the pulpit. A gloriously carved oaken one with inset panels showing biblical scenes and a great carving of a dove supporting the church bible. You reached it up a tiny staircase, where it hung some several feet off the ground.

'Have you found something?'

'No,' said Bertram. 'I was wondering if I would make a good vicar. You get quite a view from up here. I can see why some priests get a bit self-important during their sermons. The pews look pretty small from here.

'I think you would hate being a vicar,' I said. 'There's an awful of talking to people and helping them with their problems. Barely any time to have a cup of tea, let alone enjoy a cigar while you read a good book.'

Bertram tripped down the steps. 'Sounds like a dreadful life.'

'I think not, if you're called to it.'

'Must be why they call it a vocation,' said Bertram. 'I will take the left pews if you take the right. Can you bend down in that dress?' Fitzroy, I thought, would have asked if my lacing was too tight, but Bertram would never mention such intimate matters to a lady.

'I shall manage,' I told him, though I expected it would be somewhat uncomfortable.

After a stomach-squeezing half an hour, I finished my side. We met at the font to examine our finds. Bertram dragged one of the large candles over so we could see. 'I have a lot of sweetie wrappers,' he said. 'I didn't realise people bought sweets to a wedding. It's not as if we weren't going to feed them.'

'Most of them are breath mints,' I said checking the

wrappers. 'You did have a stag night. Maybe some of your fellows were still hung over.'

'Doubt it. Hans organised a rather sober affair. Probably because the Bishop came.'

I laughed. 'I think he mistakes the character of my step-father. While he wouldn't be up for anything outrageous, I don't think he wears his clerical cloth too tightly.'

'I also found a seating arrangement. It's quite precise. I don't remember this.'

I took in and examined it in the candlelight. 'Neither do I, but it is the kind of thing my mother might do. I found another copy.' I held them up side by side. 'They are not the same.'

'Is it your mother's handwriting?'

'It's a good copperplate,' I said. 'Many people could have done it.'

'Not me. Being left-handed, I always smudged the ink across the page.'

'I didn't realise…'

'Oh, I mainly use my right hand. Used to get beaten for using my left at school. Everything's still easier with my left though.'

'Bertram, I am more than happy for you to be outwardly left-handed when we set up home together. I will tell the maids to arrange cutlery and other things accordingly.'

Bertram made a harrumphing sort of sound and then said, 'You are a jolly good sort of a girl. I am ever so glad I got up the courage to ask you to marry me.'

'I wanted you to ask me for an age,' I said. 'But I didn't know how to go about encouraging you. I only got engaged to Rory because I thought I could never be with you, and it would make things easier.'

'Silly girl,' said Bertram, and I heard the relief in his

voice. 'I almost asked you once, much earlier in our acquaintance, but I bottled out and asked you to be my housekeeper instead.'

I answered him with an embrace, and we both forgot about our search, Richard, and the rest of the world for a short while.

Chapter Eight

'We have to face the antechamber,' said Bertram.

I nodded. 'Lots of light?'

'Candelabras of light,' said Bertram. 'You hang back while I fill the place with a wax bonfire.'

I watched him carry candle after candle into the room beyond. I might not be scared of churches, but the shade of Richard Stapleford, whether manifest or in my own mind, scared me. A monster in life, I could not bring myself to imagine what devil he had become in death.

'I could get some holy water from the font?' said Bertram.

'I am not sure if you are joking.'

'Neither am I. But the place is all lit up. It's been scrubbed clean already. You wouldn't realise anything had happened in there.'

He offered me his arm and together we stepped over the threshold. Immediately I felt the temperature plummet. 'You're shivering,' said Bertram.

'It is much colder in here.'

'Not really. Those grate things in the floor pump the heat through the whole church at the same time. If anything, this room should be warmer with all the candles.'

I surveyed the room. It looked like the antechamber of any parish church. A shaft of moonlight glanced down from a small window high up on the wall opposite where we had entered. It cast a green and red image on the flagstones, but it was either mired with dirt or worn with age. The details could not be distinguished. There was a single door to the outside, bolted shut, although I could not recall whether or not it had been when I found Richard. Made of the large grey blocks of stone as the rest of the building, the antechamber had a vaulted ceiling that came to a point from which hung a grotesque. It leered down at us. The mason had carved it with its tongue sticking out and the face drawn into a ferocious grimace. The arrow-shaped end of its curled tail hung down as if might fall or strike out at any moment.

'Ugly things,' said Bertram following my gaze. 'Are they meant to ward evil away or warn us who might be tormenting us in the next life if we don't mind our Ps and Qs?'

'I don't even remember it being there,' I said.

'Maybe it is Richard,' said Bertram.

'Or maybe it has come to mark the site of the murder,' I said.

'I was joking,' said Bertram.

I gave myself a little shake. 'It is all too easy to get caught up in the gothic cold of this place. Let's split up and give the room a thorough check over. The sooner we leave the better.'

'Are you certain you do not want to search together?'

'You can hardly search with me hanging off your arm,' I said. I caught his concerned expression on his face in the candlelight. 'Ah, did you mean to do the searching yourself?' My mind immediately flew to two explanations for his behaviour; that there was something he did not wish me to find or that he wished to spare me exertion and distress. My heart told me it was the latter.

'I am well,' I said. 'The experience, although most distressing at the time, I have consigned to the past.'

Bertram gave me a disbelieving look.

I sighed. 'If you will not believe that, then allow me to

75

help see justice served.'

'That's the thing, Euphemia. Justice was served. Richard deserved what he got.'

'No single soul has the right to mete out God's justice,' I said. I heard my voice say the words, but they did not ring as true for me as they once had.

'Fair enough,' said Bertram. 'You always did have loftier principles than I.' He smiled and patted my hand. 'But if you do get frightened -' He saw my face. 'I mean, too tired, I will be happy to carry on.'

I blinked back tears. 'Are you all right, my love?' said Bertram.

'You are right. I am tired,' I said. 'Let us get this done.' I broke away and moved to the side of the room where I had found Richard. One tear escaped and I brushed it away quickly. When I had sworn myself over to Fitzroy, I felt like I had made a bargain with the devil. I never regretted my action as much as I did then.

In one corner was a pile of chairs, dusty with cobwebs. They must have been there a long time, but I did not remember them any more than I had the carving on the ceiling. I realised that the drama of the event had distorted my memory. But the state of them convinced me that nothing had been disturbed in that corner. In front of me stood an inky square of darkness. Someone had stood up the screen again. I picked up one of the candles Bertram had brought through and stepped behind the screen. A shape on the floor stopped me in my tracks.

For a heart stopping moment I thought Richard's body still lay on the ground. I quickly realised it was too small. I crouched down bringing the light closer and almost vomited as I saw blood. I rocked back on my heels and had to put out a hand to save myself. Someone had indeed been sent to

76

clean the chamber, for here was the pile of rags they had used. Either Hans' servants had become lazy or, I thought more calmly, left them here until a fire could be lit discreetly outside to dispose of them.

I swallowed the bile in my throat. I placed the candlestick down away from the bloody spectacle and put out my right hand to gain purchase enough to rise.[10] My fingers slid through the floor. I jerked back and sat down heavily. At the same time, I heard Bertram sneeze. 'Bless you,' I called.

'Than-a-choo you,' said Bertram. 'Almost done. Anything over there?'

'Not yet,' I lied. I moved the candlestick once more, so it was closer to where my right hand had been. As Bertram had mentioned, there was a line of curious little grates running parallel to the wall. That, in itself, did not interest me, but as my fingers had gone through the grating, they had felt something. Though I was loath to be on knees, and at the mercy of whatever still lingered here, I switched to all fours and poked the fingers of both hands down through the grating. Something had brushed my fingers. Something that did not feel like a pipe. I only hoped that the mousing and ratting cats Hans kept did a decent job.

Again, I felt something out of place. My index finger traced the edge. There was so much dust in the grate that I dared not bring the flame closer. In a few moments my fingers told me it was a small curled pocket book. The owner had rolled it up to pass it through the grate, but once there the pages had partially uncurled. I tried to lift the grate and a small section came away easily.

Bertram sneezed violently several times. 'You know, old

---

[10]Men's garments are far easier for such an endeavour and I struggled in my attire.

girl, I think this is no good. Silly idea of ours in the first place.'

'One more minute,' I called from behind the screen. 'I do not wish to return just yet.'

'No indeed,' said Bertram. 'Must ensure we do a thorough search.' I heard him moving about on the other side of the screen. He could not be far from me.

Carefully, and with a necessary slowness that sent prickles of sweat down my back, I managed to reach the book and started to pull it up. I almost had it when Bertram sneezed once more, startling me and I dropped it. This time it went further down, and I was forced to more or less lie along the floor to give my fingers the best distance and angle for purchase. This time I only hooked it with my index finger. I pulled it slowly up, all the time feeling it wobble on my fingertip and reached my other hand down to steady it.

'Think I'm done, old girl,' said Bertram. 'Need any help?'

For a few moments the pocketbook, my fingers and the grating seemed to be permanently intertwined as I hurried to get it and replace the metal plate.

'Euphemia? Is anything wrong?'

'No,' I called, scrambling to my feet. I tucked the pocket book into my cleavage and quickly swept the edges of my poor skirt across the floor, so there were no signs of my activity. Bertram folded back the edge of the screen. 'Oh, how ghastly,' he said, seeing the rags. 'You should have let me...'

'I am not a fragile flower, Bertram. You should know that by now.'

'Indeed not, my love,' said Bertram sweeping me into his arms. I heard the papers rustle in my bodice, but the noise was lost to another of Bertram's sneezes. 'Good heavens, but you are dusty. We must get a maid to run you a hot bath.'

'We must put everything back,' I said. 'Or it will be known we were here.'

'We didn't find anything,' pointed out Bertram.

'It's only polite,' I said.

'I suppose you have a point,' said Bertram glumly. 'I'll do that if you head off for that bath. Probably better we don't come sneaking back in together. Besides, there is no way I can kiss you when you are this dirty.'

'Ridiculous, is it not? If things had gone as they should we would have been married for almost two days and climbing into bed together would be the most natural thing in the world.'

'Euphemia! You're not suggesting...?'

Even with the light of so many candles, I could not read the expression on his face. His tone was astonished, but whether it was happy astonishment or disapproval, I could not tell. 'No. No, of course not,' I said. 'We will wed soon enough.'

'Oh, I see. For a moment I thought... Well, never mind. I have hated my brother for as long as I remember,' said Bertram, 'and now I find I hate him a little more.'

Would I have gone with him then to his bedchamber? I do not know. My world had been turned on its head and of all the things that remained good and true, I knew it was the love between us. Would it have been so very terrible to have sought comfort in his arms? My moral compass, once my steadfast guide, spun in confusion.

I walked back to the house. Once I had bathed, a terrible weariness overcame me. I could barely keep my eyes open long enough to stagger to my bed. I kept the pocketbook under my pillow. Tomorrow, I told myself, I would share its discovery with Bertram. If I could not trust him, how could I trust anyone.

The next morning saw me up and dressed early enough to be the first down to breakfast. I had stowed the pocketbook at my breast, unopened. Bertram, I knew, needed sufficient tea and toast to rouse himself to full wakefulness. Stone looked a little startled to see me up so early, but he quickly brought me toast to add to the range of breakfast foods in the multitude of warming dishes that lay along the sideboard. I discovered I felt remarkably hungry and stoked my plate higher than I might have done in company. I sat down to eat with some relish. In the distance I heard the ring of the doorbell. It was far too early for callers. I presumed it must be either a new or a particularly precocious tradesman. I listened for the quiet thunder of Stone's voice. It didn't come. Instead, a few minutes later, Stone stood at the doorway to the breakfast room, coughed uneasily. 'The police, miss,' he said. 'The *gentleman* assured me you would be eager to see him.' Before he could further his explanation a tall man in a driving coat brushed past him. He drew off his driving gloves and dropped them down beside the plate next to mine. Then he shrugged himself out of his coat and threw it down on the next chair, warding off Stone's attempt to take it with a stern hand.

'You don't mind if I help myself to some breakfast, do you, Miss Martins?' said Fitzroy, grinning down at me. 'I had to be away rather early to get here at a reasonable time.'

'It is fine, Stone,' I said. 'Perhaps you could tell Mr Muller that the police are here again?'

'Oh, no need to do that,' said Fitzroy. He already had his plate in hand and was spooning mushrooms onto it. 'I won't be here a trice. Better to not upset the household again. They've been through a lot. Just a couple of formalities I need to go over with Miss Martins.'

'Miss?' said Stone.

'The gentleman is right,' I said. 'If he is departing soon,' I gave the growing pile on Fitzroy's plate a dark look, 'it may be for the best to leave the others undisturbed.'

'As you wish, miss.' Stone left closing the door behind him silent disapproval.

Fitzroy sat down with a truly enormous amount of food in front of him. He saw me looking at it incredulously and grinned again. 'When I'm short on sleep I always find I get the most tremendous hunger,' he said. 'By the way, I assume they do now know you're Miss Martins and not Miss St John?'

'I hadn't thought…' I said. 'Stone would not comment.'

'Like name, like nature?'

'Something like that. What do you want, Fitzroy?'

'Why, you, of course.'

Chapter Nine

'I cannot simply leave without a word again!'
Fitzroy shrugged and pressed on with his food.

'My family were distressed enough before. Rory did not even tell them I had gone with you. Bertram worked it out by a gardener's description.'

'Which was?' said the spy through a mouthful of scrambled egg.

'I have no idea,' I snapped.

'Shame,' said Fitzroy cutting up a sausage. 'Always interesting to learn how others perceive you. Eat up. We have a bit of drive ahead of us.'

'But I can't!' I repeated.

'My dear Alice,' said Fitzroy with a return to his sterner self, 'You do not have a choice. I say jump and you jump. That is how this works.'

'But it will look odd.'

'Perhaps, but I find myself with unexpectedly free time today, and as I had been feeling a little uncomfortable about returning you to a house wherein there might be a murderer, I thought it was about time I made good on my promise to teach you some self-defence. Not going to get a lot done in a day, but we might manage enough to save your life.'

'I see. So, I will be returning this afternoon?'

'In time for dinner,' said Fitzroy. 'I am rather caught up in something, as I think I explained to you.'

'Not really,' I said. 'Still, I suppose I can suggest there are some details about the investigation that need to be worked out - or something.'

Fitzroy nodded. 'You must ask the cook what she adds to these mushrooms. They are remarkable. But, yes, ends that need tidying up is always a good excuse. Why did you tell them you had been away?'

'Much the same,' I said. 'But I let them put it together.'

. Fitzroy nodded and stuffed a grilled tomato into his face. If I didn't know better, I would think he hadn't eaten for days. His manners were barely on the right side of acceptable. 'Excellent. Always better to let people answer their own questions. Lies are too easily found out. And they get far too complicated.'

'You speak from experience?' I said, smiling. Then I remembered. 'I apologise. I did not mean to be rude.'

Fitzroy appropriated someone else's napkin to wipe his mouth. 'Never mind that. I've been having a bit of a think about you and me. We haven't got it right yet, have we? We can discuss it in the car. Get your coat and don't let anyone see you. You can leave a message with Granite-face.'

'Stone.'

'Whatever. Now hurry up, Alice.'

'Do I need anything?'

'Only your wits and a sense of balance. I'll meet you in the lobby.'

I left a short message with the butler. Stone, notoriously stoic and unresponsive, asked me to repeat the message, so he was quite certain he understood. I felt like a small child trying to explain to their headmaster why their homework is in the dog and not on their desk. Without so much as him cracking a facial expression I was left in no doubt that his opinion of me had sunk a great deal lower – even lower than when I had been accused of murder. After all, I was leaving him to make my excuses to a group of people who would be justifiably outraged at my second disappearance.

Fitzroy shot out the door and pulled his car round to the front. I got in and tied my hat with a scarf underneath my chin. It is not the most flattering of looks but having almost lost one hat before, I had determined to ensure I did not lose this one. Once satisfied, I settled down in my seat lost in thought.

Sometime later, I cannot say where or when I was, so much absorbed by my thoughts, Fitzroy broke in on them, 'Don't sulk, Alice. Your family will forgive you. A day's unexpected absence is a small thing in the scheme of things.'

I shook myself slightly and turned to look at him. 'I did not mean to appear to sulk. I was lost in my thoughts. Besides, don't you need all your concentration to drive this fast?'

'Hardly. Glorious day and a clear open road. They don't seem to go in for hills here much.'

'No,' I said. 'Though it is not as bad as the Fens.'

'Your ultimate destination?'

I nodded.

'You've seen White Orchards, haven't you? Do you dislike it so much?'

'I will struggle to think of it as home – or I would, if Bertram were not to be there.'

'You have made up?'

'Yes, but that didn't stop me considering whether or not he was the murderer when he offered to search the church with me last night.'

'Did you let him?'

'Yes, but I took the part where the murder occurred.'

'A decent compromise.'

'Yes, but the thought that I could suspect him made me uncomfortable. I have been having a lot of uncomfortable thoughts.'

Fitzroy turned to look at me and my heart almost stopped, as he only glanced back at the road in time, or so it seemed, to make the bend. 'I expect you have,' he said. 'Was that what you were thinking about? If so, I acquit you of sulking. Adjustment to this side of the looking glass is not easy.'

'I believe I have begun to think like you.'

'From my perspective that is an excellent thing. Not so much from yours, I presume.'

'If I ever had a moral compass, I feel it is spinning and freefalling at the same time.'

Fitzroy kept his eyes on the road, but I saw his wry smile spread across his face. 'What a charming image of me you must have.'

'I didn't mean -'

He interrupted. 'Bertram will be your moral compass. He can return the favour.'

'I'm sorry.'

'Didn't you once tell me that it was your strictures that made Bertram wake up to the idea of giving justice a helping hand if it was in his capabilities – and even that he should stop sponging off the blood money of his family?'

'Which is when he ran off and bought White Orchards,' I said miserably. 'Not a tale that ends well.'

Fitzroy gave a little chuckle. 'You made him a better man and he will keep you a better woman – or at least a better person than me.'

'What about you? Who is your moral lodestone?'

'I did not have one before I met you.' He grinned. 'See what a responsibility you have, Alice - you have to ensure I stay within the bounds of decent human behaviour.'

'I don't see how I can do that,' I said tartly, 'when I am not allowed to speak my mind.'

I expected him to snap at me, but the grin softened to a

smile. 'That's what I have been thinking about. We are friends, aren't we, Alice?'

'We were.'

'Before I got all heavy-handed about being your trainer, you mean?'

I kept silent.

'Well, your unspoken criticism is well founded. This is the first time for me that an asset, who has also become a friend, has become my trainee. You have so little experience of my world, and there are so many pitfalls, I constantly fear - perhaps wrongly - that you will tumble into one and do yourself real harm.'

'Are you staying you are trying to protect me?'

'In a roundabout sort of way. Shall we agree you can speak with me much as you once did when we are alone, but in the presence of other agents you will show at least a modicum of respect towards me.'

'And if the situation is ever difficult, I will follow your directions without question,' I added.

'Thank you,' said Fitzroy. 'Am I forgiven?'

'You always manage to get me to forgive you,' I said grumpily. 'No matter what you've done. However, I do admit I missed having someone with whom I could talk about anything – you remember promising me that years ago?'

'Of course, but you have Bertram.'

'Yes, and much as I adore him, there are countless subjects that I could never see myself raising with him.'

'You should work on that,' said Fitzroy seriously. 'Now, tell me everything that happened, as much as you can recall, from your time at Muller's estate.'

'There isn't much.'

'Maybe not, but I want to see how your ability to observe

is improving as well as your ability to report coherently.'

I told him in nauseating detail what had happened. He laughed at Hans' dilemma. 'To think I used to believe he was a halfway decent human being,' said Fitzroy. 'It's almost reassuring to learn he is just like the rest.'

I continued on. At the end of my tale he asked me, 'Two things stand out for me. Obviously, I want to see that notebook, but who was the guest your mother referred to?'

'I assume one of the wedding guests. Or a friend of the Bishop.'

Fitzroy tut-tutted. 'Never assume, Alice. Things nearly always go to the bad when one does.'

A while back we had turned into a network of country lanes. I had been too taken by our conversation to pay attention to where we were, but when I looked out over the fields, I saw no familiar landmarks. The spy steered the car down a narrow tree-lined track and pulled up outside a large old Tudor-beamed farmhouse. He shut off the motor and jumped out.

'This is it,' he said, leaving me to scramble down on my own. 'Let's go in and see who is around.'

He opened the front door and entered yelling, 'How now!' There was no immediate response. I followed him into a dim hallway, surrounded by doors with a staircase leading up on the right. 'Go through that door, Alice,' he said pointing. 'And take off your hat. Never wear anything around your neck. It's asking for trouble.'

I went forward, hoping there would be a mirror somewhere in this strange, quiet farmhouse. Fitzroy ran up the stairs. I thought I heard him mutter to himself, 'Got to be someone…' Then he was gone. I opened the door and found myself in the oddest room. In it stood not one single stick of furniture. Nothing hung on the walls. The only noticeable aspect of the room was the pale, woven matting under my feet that spread across the entirety of the room. A large window at the back gave out onto a small copse and afforded some much-needed light. Making do with what little I had, I used my reflection in the window glass to unpin my hat. Of course, this meant my hair tumbled down. I could have been no more than half way through re-pinning it when Fitzroy returned towing a younger man behind him. 'This is Cole,' he said. 'I trained him. He's agreed to give us some time.'

Cole moved forward into the window's light. I thought he would offer his hand, but he did not and so I did not offer mine. Fitzroy turned to shut the door behind. 'Quiet as the grave here today,' he said.

Cole studied me openly, so I returned the favour. Slightly less tall than Fitzroy, he had a slender build and jet-black hair. He was clean-shaven and did not sport even the smallest of moustaches. His eyes were of a strange, sparkling blue that shone with an intensity I found disturbing. Not least because they were entirely cold. His lips were thin and pink, his cheekbones high, and his chin and neck well-formed. He was one of the most handsome men I had ever seen, but I did not find him in the least attractive. Every hair on my body stood on end and every instinct told me to run. Cole gave me a tiny, unfriendly smile – quite as though he could read my thoughts.

'As I was saying, Cole, this can't be one of our typical training exercises. The Suffragettes have been using jujitsu to remarkable effect. I think a basic variant on that, don't you?' He looked at me. 'We have two things to consider. On the negative side, if you were ever attacked, Alice, it is likely you would be dressed as you are now. Both Cole and I are considerably less constrained by our clothing and have a multitude of defence manoeuvres available to us that I do not think you would find possible. On the positive side, unless you are marching in Suffragette colours, and perhaps not even then, men don't, in the general scheme of things, expect women to fight back. Fast, simple responses that allow you to escape the situation are our first best option.'

'She will need to cause them pain.'

'Not necessarily,' said Fitzroy. 'There are some men who pain emboldens. We can assume,' here he turned and slyly winked at me, 'that any man who attacks a woman is not typical of our gender.'

'Or is a thug or spy,' said Cole. 'Someone who knows all too well what they are doing.'

'Exactly,' said Fitzroy, 'We don't have that long, so while I would prefer you did not break Alice, I do not want you to go easy on her.'

'As if I would,' said Cole. Fitzroy laughed, but I felt a spasm of fear shoot through me.

'Right, let's start,' said Fitzroy. 'Watch us, Alice, and then you get to repeat my part with Cole.'

'Don't you need to be wearing a skirt for this, boss?' said Cole.

'I have an excellent imagination,' said Fitzroy, entirely unruffled. 'Now come at me and try and choke me.'

Cole marched up and took Fitzroy by the throat. Immediately the spy pushed his two hands together up and out through Cole's arms, breaking his grip. He then brought his outstretched arms down on each side of Cole's head. 'At this point,' he said, 'you clap your hands over his ears as hard and fast as you can. It's called a thunderclap for obvious reasons. Often breaks their eardrums. Come here and copy what I did, but don't actually deafen Cole.' He stepped back.

I moved forward and before I could even signal my assent

Cole had his hands tight around my neck. His blue eyes stared unflinchingly into mine. I wanted to cry out that the grip was too strong, but I could not speak. My vision began to swim.

'Anytime, Alice,' said Fitzroy. I realised he did not know how hard Cole held me in his grip. I pushed my arms up and through his, breaking the grip, and stopped short of clapping my hands over his ears by no more than an inch. I stepped back breathing heavily. More than anything I was astonished I had broken his grip.

'Good first attempt,' said Fitzroy. 'Go again.'

We continued in this vein until Fitzroy felt I was fluent in the move. 'It's a start. Cole, here. Choke me.'

Cole did as he was bid. Fitzroy turned his body, lowering it slightly as he brought his right arm crashing down on Cole's arms. Then he somehow trapped Cole's left arm, and using this, flipped him onto his front on the ground, still holding the left arm, which he forced up towards Cole's shoulder until he tapped twice on the ground. Fitzroy released him and stepped back. 'That's the next stage,' he said. 'We don't have time to do that today, but I wanted you to see that we are showing you basic building blocks of self-defence that can be built into more sophisticated moves that even allow you to trap and hold your assailant.'

'What if someone grabs my neck from behind?' I asked.

'Ah, there's a nice easy one for that. Cole?'

Cole's expression grew somewhat resigned. He put his arm around Fitzroy's neck and pulled backwards. The spy dropped his weight and threw Cole over his head. Cole landed on the mat but rolled neatly to a standing position.

Fitzroy gave me an apologetic look. 'Can't teach you how to fall dressed like that, I'm afraid. But do try your luck throwing Cole. He's not that heavy.'

I tried, but I could not shift him. The move was nowhere near as easy as Fitzroy made it look. On my tenth failed attempt, Fitzroy sighed. 'Stop. Stop. You're not getting it. I think we need to go back to something more basic.'

'Break, stun, and run, boss?' said Cole.

Fitzroy nodded. 'OK. Cole, choke me.' Cole repeated the action of putting his arm around Fitzroy's neck. 'Right,' said Fitzroy, 'first you stamp down as hard as you can on his instep – here.' He stood on Cole's foot, but did not stamp. 'If you wanted to be clever you scrape the edge of your shoe down his leg as you do it. Then you put your head back sharply.' He moved his head back slowly. 'You're aiming to break his nose. It will hurt the back of your head, but not as much as it hurts his nose. Then run. Got it?'

'I think so,' I said. 'But what happens if he picks me up off my feet.'

'Raise your leg and go for the knee,' said Cole. 'It takes only a few of pounds of pressure to make it bend the other way.' He flashed another grin at me. His eyes remained as cold and dead as ever.

'Come and have a go,' said Fitzroy. 'I didn't you show you this first because it's all done in slow motion. You're not actually trying to hurt your partner. It's not the same as practising something in real time.'

I managed to repeat the move successfully, several times. 'Good enough,' said Fitzroy. 'Let's hope you remember to do it faster if you ever need to use it.'

We continued in this vein for some time. Fitzroy showed me how to break out from a hand grip by putting pressure against the thumb when pulling away. He and Cole ran through the weak spots that took only a minimal amount of force to be effectively damaged. 'One that works well for women is to grab the lower lip tightly and drop to the floor.

Bit bloody, but still…'

'I like the way people follow their ears, boss,' said Cole. 'Grab them and twist the head. Very dramatic.'

Fitzroy shook his head. 'Let's not get carried away. Alice is going to be shorter than most men she encounters. Probably an idea to give you some basic stick training.'

'I don't carry a stick,' I said.

'Most men do,' said Cole, 'and it's surprising how few have learned to use them.'

'Even if you are not in a position to take the cane away from your opponent,' said Fitzroy, 'knowing what it is possible with it will help you evade it. I think we should move on to dodging and evading after lunch.'

'Only bread and cheese in the kitchen, boss.'

'Well, that will do for you. I've got stuff in the car for us. Take her through to the kitchen and I'll bring it in.'

Fitzroy disappeared off. 'This way,' said Cole leading me back into the hallway. Behind him, in the dimly lit lobby, I rubbed my throat. He'd used a hard grip on me, and it felt tender. I pulled my collar up tightly.

The kitchen looked like an average farmhouse one except for its cleanliness. I sat down in a chair at the large wooden table and waited for Fitzroy. 'Are you not going to make my sandwich?' said Cole.

'Leaving aside that I have never been here before and do not know where things are kept, I quite simply wouldn't know how, 'I said. 'Fitzroy did not recruit me for my domestic abilities.'

Cole looked me up and down several times and I felt myself blushing. 'I bet he didn't,' he said. 'So, what are your particular skills? Are you going to be his right hand?' He leered when he said this. I did not understand what he meant, and was debating what to say when Fitzroy came in.

'No,' said the spy. 'She has an unusually quick mind, responds calmly in a crisis and is utterly loyal to me.' A look passed between the two men I could not fathom except Cole became slightly chagrinned. Fitzroy lightened his tone. 'Hasn't a clue how to feed herself, have you, Alice?'

'No,' I said, matching his lighter tone, 'but I clean a mean staircase.'

Fitzroy laughed. 'Don't tell Cole that. There are more stairs in this old house than I care to count, and someone has to clean them.'

'I'm guessing you do not use servants here either,' I said.

'No indeed,' said Fitzroy as he emptied out bread, cheeses, pâtés, fruit, and wine onto the table.

'This line of work does not tend to suit people from the upper classes,' said Cole.

Fitzroy and I looked at each other and both laughed. Cole's face grew darker.

'Eat up,' said Fitzroy. 'We don't have much time left. I don't want to do the first part of the drive in the dark. I swear the trees around here move.'

Cole laughed. 'We got the dents out, didn't we, boss?' I looked over at Fitzroy, horrified that my first judgement of his driving might have been correct. The spy avoided my eye.

We spent the afternoon repeating what I had learned in the morning, learning what Fitzroy called joint locks and how to avoid them. By the time he called it a day I was extremely tired and very sore. The spy sent me out to the car, while he 'finished up' at the farmhouse. I re-pinned my hat and wound the scarf around my neck. Only a few minutes later the spy came out. He started the car and lit the lamps even though we still had a little daylight left.

He climbed in. 'So, what did you make of Cole?'

'I assume you also trained him, but I am afraid I would not care to be in his company alone.'

'Right on both counts.' He took in my appearance. 'You seem quite calm after all that. Good to see. It's not every woman who can...' he stopped and reached out to tug at my scarf. I put up my hand to stop him. 'I thought I told you never to wear things around your neck...' Then he spotted the bruising. 'Bloody hell,' he said. 'Why didn't you tell him he was hurting you?'

'He knew,' I said.

'Then why didn't you tell me?'

I shrugged.[11] 'It is not very sore. I thought I was meant to take it.'

'Part of a test, you mean?' said Fitzroy. 'Good Lord, what you must think of me? Yes, there might be times, much later on in your training, when I... you say he knew he was hurting you?'

I nodded.

'Wait here.' He got out the car and disappeared back into the farmhouse. He returned a few moments later cradling his right hand. He gave it a shake and got into the car. As he pulled on his driving gloves I noticed the skin on the knuckles on his right hand was broken and bloody.

'You should get some ice for that,' I said.

'Later. We have delayed too long.' He drove off. I sat quietly thinking about what he had done. I suspected from the grim look on Fitzroy's face my thanks would not be welcome. Finally, to break the silence as much as anything, I asked, 'What is Cole's specialism?'

'Assassination,' said Fitzroy in a level tone.

We drove on in silence. I had little to share and much to

---

[11] A bad habit of his I had managed to acquire.

think about. We stopped at a four-way junction and I roused myself to look around. 'I don't recognise this,' I said. 'Are we lost?'

'No, but I can't take you back to the Mullers now, can I?'

'I don't understand.'

'How would you explain to Bertram about the bruising on your throat?'

'Oh,' I said.

'And don't try and tell me he'd miss it. You know as well as I do, the moment you're back with him you'll be... well, it's nothing to do with me, but he'll notice.'

'Kissing,' I said. 'He kisses me. So yes, he would notice.'

'I don't need details,' said the spy.

'There's nothing more to tell,' I said.

'How would you explain it? He'd never let you go anywhere with me again.'

'Bertram does not control my actions now, nor will he when we are married.'

'And he knows this?'

'Of course.'

'Then you have found yourself a remarkable man. But you see the predicament. I'm still on an operation, but I think you might be useful. It's not mine. I'm only helping out. The chap running it hasn't thought it through, and I think you might be able to offer us a way out of the deadlock we've reached.'

'How?' I asked.

'Seduction,' said Fitzroy quite calmly.

Chapter Ten

I quelled my impulse to jump out of the speeding car while shouting 'What kind of female do you think I am?'

I did this for two reasons. Firstly, I had no knowledge of how to leap out of a vehicle and land avoiding potentially mortal damage, and secondly, I had become accustomed to Fitzroy's occasional, and somewhat evil, sense of humour. I decided to assume he did not mean exactly what he said.

I furrowed my brow and said calmly, 'I seem to recall you once telling me you had an affair with a European princess to gain intelligence.'

Fitzroy nodded. 'The things I've had to do for our country.'

Were it not for the fact that I knew it was impossible, I would have thought my heart had dropped down into my boots.

'Oh,' I said, still hoping he was playing some kind of game.

'Actually, she was very nice. Pretty too. I'd write, but I don't think her family would like it. Germans, you see.'

I sighed. 'You are not suggesting I sacrifice my virginity to a stranger, are you? A moment ago, you were punching your previous trainee in the face because he had bruised me. This seems to me to be much more serious.'

'He overstepped the mark,' said Fitzroy. 'Besides, Cole has always needed a firm hand to keep him in line. Unfortunately, there was no one else at the farm today.'

'I take it the farmhouse is a sort of club house for British spies?'

Fitzroy laughed. 'It's lacking a few of the finer amenities of the London Clubs, but essentially, yes.'

He lapsed into silence without answering my question. I decided he was definitely teasing me. A while later he said, 'We're going to have to do something about your clothes.'

'I don't have any. You said we would only be away for a day.'

'This is hardly my fault,' objected the spy.

'Of course not,' I said trying to placate him. 'I could try and find…'

'No time for faffing about.'

'What do you suggest?'

'We'll have to steal some. Always a bit hit and miss stealing women's clothing. You come in such a vast arrangement of sizes and wear such different styles. I think we will only have time to get a couple. You'll have to make the best of it.'

'So now I am to be a thief as well as a seductress?'

Fitzroy flashed me a grin. 'Aren't you having an exciting day?' When I did not smile back, he said, 'You can stay in the car with the engine running. I think it's better I do the actual lifting. You would probably get caught.'

'Why do you say that?' I said stung.

'Oh, you'd doubtless be overcome by some moral qualm at a key moment and freeze.'

'Whereas you have no qualms at all.'

'I do have my own code,' said the spy, 'but I doubt you would consider it moral. You, on the other hand, are terribly hindered by morals. Don't worry, Alice, I'll train you out of them.'

I gave up and fell into silence. I was not going to get any sense out of the dratted man. But if he thought he could get me to sacrifice my virtue then he had a vase over the head coming. I glanced askance and caught him grinning at me. I averted my face and he gave a bark of laughter but entered into no further conversation.

I realised we were headed London-wards. I doubted we could make the metropolis tonight, but I was surprised when Fitzroy pulled into the backyard of a respectable, but not exclusive, inn. He gestured to me to stay put and jumped out. Moments later, he returned carrying a pink striped case that he threw in the back before hopping with some alacrity back into the driver's seat. 'Your first set, Alice.'

I could not help looking behind us to see if anyone had noticed this theft, but the road stayed quiet. 'Took it from what I think was the arrivals area, so hopefully it's full of clean clothes. I doubt you know how to wash any.'

'I can wash clothing,' I said coldly.

'Good to know. I'll remember that if we stay holed up at the Mews again.'

I bit my lip and determined to not to say another word before we reached our destination. The more I said the worse this got. Fitzroy stopped once more and acquired a blue case. Again, the owner appeared to be paying no attention to their luggage. We drove on for a while. Then he pulled into a siding. 'I'm going to rearrange things in the back, so it looks like it was packed deliberately. 'If you look in the pouch fitted to the door you should find something we need.'

I put my hand in the opening and discovered a series of things: a half-eaten apple, a pocket knife, a small mirror, a box of matches, and a plain gold ring. I heard the luggage being shifted behind me then he climbed back into the driver's seat. We were now well into twilight, but he could see well enough. 'Ah, you found it. I was a bit worried it might have fallen out the bottom. I should have kept it in the box.'

'The apple,' I said stupidly.

'The ring. Put it on.'

Confused, I slipped the ring onto my finger. It fitted well.

'Left hand,' said Fitzroy. 'Third finger.'

'You cannot be serious,' I said.

'Indeed, I am, Mrs Fitzroy. There is no way we can arrive to stay at a respectable establishment without being wed.'

I swallowed and changed the ring to my wedding finger. He was right. Unless we claimed to be brother and sister, and there was not an ounce of family resemblance, we would be turned away at the door.

'Oh, I'm not using Fitzroy. Our surname is Brown. Nice and forgettable.' He patted my arm. 'Poor Alice. Do exactly as I tell you and everything will be fine. With luck we shall even enjoy a good dinner without have to cook it ourselves!'

'I am confused.'

'I know. You have to trust me. That's all I ask. If you give me the notebook you found later, I'll have a look through it. If it is Richard's, I can't imagine that he would write anything in it uncoded. But as he wasn't the brightest spark that shouldn't be an issue.' He gave a modest little smile. 'I'm rather good with codes. Aren't you lucky?'

'Unbelievably lucky,' I said grimly. This made him laugh again.

'Almost there now,' he said. 'You'll like it.'

It would have been hard not to like the hotel. A discreet distance from London, it nevertheless excelled in luxury. 'The conference has taken over the whole place,' said Fitzroy as we got out of the car. He offered me his arm. 'Now, Mrs Brown, pretend that this is a great treat. I've only brought you along because I accidentally ran over your cat. There are a number of other attendees with spouses, so you won't be out of place.'

'What was it called?'

Fitzroy stopped. 'What was what called?'

'The cat,' I said.

'Lazarus,' said the spy and began walking again.

'Very funny. What is this conference about?'

'Nothing a wife needs to worry her pretty little head about. Smile and be charming. No opinions and certainly don't say anything in the least bit clever. You're too young for us to have had children – so you're my second wife and step-mother to Nicolas, who is an absolute darling, if something of a scamp. He's six and you hate it when I thrash him.'

'Would you thrash a child?' I asked.

'No, of course not. But Mr Brown would. Got it? You can embroider if you want but ensure it's nothing anyone would ask me about. You know, how charmingly you've set up the nursery and your wonderful cook. All the sorts of things ladies gabble about.'

'I don't gabble.'

'Well then you're in for a steep learning curve.'

By this time, we had reached the desk. Fitzroy signed us both in and was given his room key. He asked for tea to be sent up for me and for three newspapers in the morning.

'Very good, sir,' said the clerk. 'Tonight, supper is at eight. Will madam be attending?'

Fitzroy assented. I realised that neither of these men had made any effort to consult me. I did my best to look sweet and a little dim. We were on the ground floor and by the time we had reached the room our bags were already waiting for us. Fitzroy tipped the porter and declined the services of a maid to unpack. When the door closed behind him, he said, 'Have you got toothache? You're pulling the strangest face.'

I explained my attempt at my unnatural expression.

'Don't do it,' said the spy. 'Just smile and say as little as possible. Maybe gush occasionally about flowers or babies or some such nonsense. That will ensure most of the men stay as far away from you as possible. Now, if you excuse me, I'm going to have a quick brush up and go and see how the land lies. Have your tea then see what you can cobble together from these cases.'

Tea came on a silver tray with crustless cucumber sandwiches and tiny little cakes.[12] I gulped down the tea and devoured the food. Doubtless Mrs Brown would have only nibbled a little, but no one was here to see, and I was ravenous. I hoped supper would prove to be substantial. I pushed to the back of my mind Fitzroy's comment about my seducing someone. Over the last couple of days, he had developed the uncomfortable habit of alternately telling me the truth and teasing me. I often found myself feeling all at sea. But he had yet to ask me to do anything truly awful, so I decided that he either wanted me to charm information from someone – presumably another wife, who I could bond with over nursery wallpaper – or he wanted me to get a gentleman away from the group, but no doubt a story of a lost ear-ring or pendant would suffice to lure him away.

By the time Fitzroy returned I was wearing a striped green skirt with a smart ruffled blouse. I had found that the upper half of the lady with the blue case resembled mine, while the pink case lady's contents fitted elsewhere. I was checking my hair in the mirror when he opened the door.

'Very nice. Now take it off.'

I whirled round to see an expression of mild annoyance on his face. 'Supper, Alice. Supper.'

---

[12]So tiny in fact I believe Richenda would have put them all in her mouth at once and even swallowed without chewing.

'Of course,' I said, blushing deeply. 'I –' I stopped, for there was no reason to go into how the various ladies did and did not resemble my figure. 'I will look again.'

Fitzroy put a small parcel he was carrying down on the bed and began to rummage through the pink case. He held up a rather resplendent, and daring, black and gold evening dress. 'What about this?'

'It won't fit,' I said.

'We don't have time to be picky, Alice. Try it.'

I could feel the blood pounding in my cheeks. 'Honestly, it won't. Whoever owned this case had a less – err – full upper figure.'

Fitzroy gave what for all the world sounded like a snigger. 'And the other one?'

'Fine on the top.'

'But not on the bottom?'

At these words I would have rushed from the room, if he had not been standing between the door and me. As it was, I fled into the en suite. Behind me I heard the spy breaking into laughter. I closed the door firmly and washed my face with cold water. About five or ten minutes later[13] there was a knock at the door. 'I've got something for you,' said the spy. I opened the door and before I could say anything, he thrust some garments into my hands. 'You'll need to wear the evening shawl with this, but it should be just enough to cover your modesty. There's a choker to cover up those bruises.' He closed the door with himself on the outside. 'Make it quick,' he said. 'I have something to show you.'

The dress he had thrown at me was a deep cobalt blue with a low back. The front décolleté was enough to have made my mother swoon, but it did allow me room for my

---

[13]Though at the time it felt like an eternity.

personage. Not quite enough room, but I could arrange the light shawl over it. I searched in the bathroom cabinet and saw that we had been left, among other things, complementary pins. I carefully secured the shawl to an effect that I felt was both elegant and would not get me carted away for lewd behaviour. Admittedly, it was a close call, but this was a private event.

I took a deep breath and opened the door. Fitzroy was adjusting his bow-tie in the mirror. I had never seen him in dinner dress before. He must have gone elsewhere to shave, or the hotel had a resident barber. Not only was he now clean-shaven, but his hair was for once firmly and neatly in place. His suit, obviously cut by an excellent tailor, fitted him perfectly. If I hadn't already given my heart to Bertram, I might have been mildly impressed at the figure he cut. I contented myself with saying, 'Very smart.'

Fitzroy, on the other hand, showed no such restraint. He turned and considered me from my toes to my hair. Then he gave a low whistle. 'I say, Alice. You do look rather the thing tonight. I'm almost envious of our quarry. That dress is perfect for the operation.'

'It is about time you told me what I am to do.'

'There is a man here. His name isn't important. He is unmissable and he has a reputation for a roving eye.' He coughed. 'Rather more than a roving eye in fact. I have no doubt he will head your way. He is slightly taller than me, with slightly longer than is fashionable blond hair and an overly tanned complexion with a slightly sallow tinge. His features are fair enough. Some women might find him handsome – square jaw, Roman nose, but rather thin lips.'

'Why won't you tell me his name?'

'One reason is when he runs into you, you will able to be genuinely say you have no idea who he is. That will sting his pride. That and your wedding ring will make you irresistible to him. Being young and an absolute knock-out, he will go all out for you.'

'All out for me?'

'To get you into bed. The dinner is big enough that he'll say you won't be missed. I imagine he'll set up some kind of diversion for me.'

'What do you want me to do?'

'Reluctantly agree to go with him to his room. As it turns out, I'm rather a brute to you.'

'I c-c-can't,' I stammered. 'I know you and the princess, but I…'

Fitzroy raised an eyebrow. 'Are you suggesting that I am immoral?' He shook his head. 'I would not ask you to sacrifice your virtue. I seem to recall saying something about looking out for you during training.' He picked up the parcel from the bed, which he had opened. He handed me a small evening bag. 'Don't open it, yet. Inside is a lady's handkerchief soaked in chloroform. All you need to do it get that to his face and he'll be out like a light. Then you open the door and I'll be waiting outside.'

'I see two problems. Firstly, you said he would arrange for a diversion for you.'

'I'm sure I will cope,' said the spy smugly.

'Secondly, you said he's taller than me. How will I reach?'

'Come on, Alice. This is serious,' He began to pace back and forth. 'This is basic stuff. There are a variety of ways. The easiest is to get him to sit down. Offer to massage his shoulders or some such feminine wile. Or jump up on his back from behind. Or tell him you'll only give him that first kiss if he closes his eyes and when he lowers his head shove the thing in his face. You need to think on your feet. If all else fails give me a shout I'll be outside, but I would far rather we did this discreetly.'

'Oh,' I said.

Fitzroy stopped pacing and regarded me. 'You've gone white as a sheet.'

'Sorry,' I said sitting down in a chair. 'I'll be alright in a minute.'

Fitzroy stalked off to the side of the room and opened a cupboard that turned out to be a hidden bar. He poured two glasses of whisky. He handed me one and downed the other in one. 'Turns out the situation is a bit more serious than when I left. I don't especially like throwing you in the deep end, but the job often goes like this. You have to think on your feet. Besides, you've got me nearby.'

I swallowed a sip of the liquid and took a deep breath. 'I will be alright. A few years ago, a man tried to rape me. I never knew who it was, but I suspected it was Richard.'

'Tried?'

'Old-fashioned chamber pots are as effective as your chloroform.'

'I didn't know,' said Fitzroy.

I shrugged. 'There is no reason why you should have done. I never told anyone. Not even Bertram.'

'If I'd been there…'

'You were,' I said. 'It was that house party…'

Fitzroy poured himself another whisky. 'I'll think of something else,' he said.

I stood up and checked my shawl was in as much order as possible. 'No, this is a fear I need to overcome.' I hesitated with my hand on the doorknob. 'Just make sure you are nearby. I'm trusting you.' And before he could protest, I slipped out of the room and headed towards the cocktail lounge to find my quarry.

Chapter Eleven

I had not taken more than a few steps when I heard the sound of gentle music and the cut glass edges of refined murmurs. I walked towards it to find a five-piece band playing at the back of a large bar. Ladies and gentlemen in smart evening dress wandered between the bar and the dance floor. If I had not known I was outside London, I might have thought we were at the Ritz. The music, the quality of the clothes, the décor, everything spoke of the highest elegance. I hesitated on the edge of the crowd, scanning the room.

'Looking for someone?' said a basso voice at my side. 'A brother perhaps? Or a father?'

I turned to see a man, much as Fitzroy had described him, standing beside me. It threw me that he had appeared so quickly. I wondered if Fitzroy's trap had already been exposed. 'My husband,' I said. I gave the words some weight but smiled slightly so as not to seem curt.

The man put his right hand on his left breast. 'Ah, you wound me to the quick. You stifle my hope so swiftly.' He had dark eyes and they glittered in the low light.

'I did not realise we were to have entertainment tonight,' I said. 'You are playing the part in some farce?'

Fitzroy would have been appalled at my behaviour, but this man for all his silly platitudes had an aura about him that made me wary. I noticed a diamond pin in his lapel. He was certainly not short of money. He carried himself with an arrogance rarely seen in an English gentleman outside of his own home. A silly simpering woman would not engage this man's interest. He was a flirt, but he was a man who wanted

106

what he could not have. I knew his type. For all Fitzroy might believe he could read his fellows, he had misread this one.

'Again, she cuts me to the quick. Another thrust to the heart.'

'I don't actually fence,' I said, 'but I do not think the manoeuvre you are describing would be possible.'

The man laughed, a genuine laugh. 'You are charming,' he said and held out his hand. 'Forgive my clumsy attempts at amusing you, I am Count von Wolff. You may call me Otto.'

I took his hand. 'It is not usual for a gentleman to introduce himself to a lady,' I said. 'But, in the spirit of international friendship, I will overlook the matter on this occasion. I am Mrs Brown. You may call me Mrs Brown.'

Instead of releasing my hand he tucked it swiftly under his arm. 'And to think I thought this evening would be interminable. Now I have met you, Mrs Brown, I have hope. Let me get you a drink. Whisky or champagne?'

'Champagne,' I said, thinking of the earlier drink that was burning holes in my stomach. I should, of course, have asked for something non-alcoholic, but then I reminded myself I did need to lead the man on a bit.

'Champagne it is,' said Otto. 'About the only good thing to ever come out of France.' The barman served him immediately to the outrage of several other couples.

'Fashion,' I said.

He handed me a glass. 'Women's fashion perhaps. I will give you that. But otherwise it is all garlic, snails, and onions.' He held his nose. I have nothing against France, or its people, but I knew I must not contradict him on anything he considered serious or I would lose him.

'Goodness,' I said. 'I do hope they are not serving French

food tonight.'

'I doubt it, my dear. I should imagine we will have good traditional English fare. So, what is your husband's interest in our meeting?'

I gave a tiny, and I hoped ladylike, shrug. 'I have no idea. I am afraid I take no interest in his affairs.'

'And yet you chose to accompany him?'

'It is meant to be a treat for me. To make up for him missing our third anniversary. And the fact he ran over my cat.' I added, the last part hastily having almost forgotten the backstory I had been given.

He smiled. 'But you do not seem to be enjoying yourself? Where is he?'

'Off talking to someone, I imagine. Quite frankly I would not be surprised if he has forgotten he has brought me along!'

I winced inwardly at this forwardness, but how else could I progress things? More discussion on food would only bore him and make me hungry.[14]

'Surely not. You look so charming tonight – and three years, it is not that long to be married.'

'I am his second wife,' I said, glad to be able to embark on the agreed history. 'His first wife died young. I have a stepson, Nile, who is six.' I couldn't for the life of me remember what we had decided the child was called. I could only hope Otto and Fitzroy did not meet.

'Ah, you have maternal duties?'

I deliberately misunderstood him. 'I like Nile very much. He is a charming child. Intelligent and mischievous. We are

---

[14] The sandwiches and cakes really had been very small. More suitable for a pigeon than a woman with a healthy appetite. On reflection Richenda wouldn't have to have even opened her mouth to consume them. She could have simply inhaled.

good friends. He does not remember his mother clearly and has accepted me.' I saw his eyes begin to glaze over and added quickly, 'In my *stepson* I have been most fortunate.'

His pupils narrowed and he tilted his head to one side. 'In your stepson, but perhaps not in other ways.'

I glanced away in an attempt to be coy, but honestly how coy could I be if Fitzroy expected me to get the man upstairs in a bedroom before we had even sat down for dinner? 'Ah well,' I said, 'all young women are romantic, are they not? We fill our heads with foolish ideas of love and passion, but the raw truth is such things only belong between the covers of a novel.'

'To be so young and so cynical. That is a great shame.'

I shrugged again, this time a little more energetically, allowing my shawl to reveal slightly more of my décolletage without it being entirely improper. I saw his gaze drop to my chest. 'Perhaps life will yet prove me wrong?' I said, lowering my voice to what I hoped was a sultry whisper.[15]

Otto placed a hand lightly on my arm. 'Would you like me to show you how wrong you are?'

Inwardly I was torn between delight that my ruse had succeeded and genuine shock that a gentleman could be so forward. Was this how all bored married women were treated? My confusion must have shown on my face.

Otto lowered his head towards me and said softly, 'If I have offended you…'

I pulled myself together. I looked up from beneath my eyelashes and felt a gentle blush heat my cheeks. 'No. It is not that. It is simply that I had not imagined that you…' I broke off, letting him fill in the rest to his own satisfaction.

---

[15] I had never before in my life had occasion to be sultry and I feared it was an act that needed practice.

A smile spread across his face. 'Go out into the lobby and climb the stairs to the first landing. Await me there. It would not do for your reputation for us to be seen leaving together.'

I decided that an embarrassed nod was the best answer to this request. I placed my glass on the table, thanked him for the drink and left the room. I walked at a reasonable pace. Fitzroy had said he would be waiting nearby. The whole plan had been delivered to me so quickly I couldn't remember the details. Did he mean near Otto's room or was he shadowing me? I wished I had taken the time to ask. There was no guarantee that Otto would take me to his room. He might have some other discreet place in mind. I inwardly cursed Fitzroy for not planning this more carefully.

I waited on the landing for no more than three minutes before Otto appeared. He nodded a greeting and offered me his arm. Then we began to ascend the stairs. 'There are so many people here I doubt that anyone will recognise you,' he said.

'And you?'

'My reputation is beyond salvaging.'

'That I cannot believe!'

He chuckled. 'You are very sweet. Have no fear, I will treat you gently.' He took a step onto the corridor of the second floor before pulling me close to him and planting a light kiss on my lips. It took all my willpower not to pull away and slap him, but then Mrs Brown had fairly blatantly asked him to do exactly this. So instead I gave a small nervous giggle. His smile widened. 'I see we understand each other. Come, my room is this way.'

I then had an awful thought. What if Fitzroy had expected me to take Otto back to our room? My heart beat a little faster. No, that was a silly idea. No man would want to sleep with someone's wife in their husband's bed. Or would they?

In my time I have had occasion to learn more about oddities of the male libido, and how they might like to satiate themselves, than most women. I had never been summoned to action, as it were, but it has been a close call more than once.[16] This unwanted knowledge made me think that Fitzroy considered that this man might go for the less safe option to heighten the excitement? However, during the few minutes in which I had known Otto and had supposedly agreed to throw my marital vows to the four winds, he did not strike me as a risk-taker. An opportunist perhaps. But the two were very different kinds of persona. Something Fitzroy would probably never understand, as he was both.

As we reached the end of the third landing, he opened a door I had taken for a room but was in reality the cover for a staircase leading upwards.

'Gosh,' I said girlishly. 'How intriguing.' Internally I quaked. I could think of several reasons for taking me up a secret staircase and in none of them did things end well – for me.

'It always pays to be discreet,' said Otto ushering me forward. 'This way, if anyone has seen us wandering along the second floor together, I can say I wanted to show you the view at the great window at the end of that landing.'

'I did not notice one,' I said, mentally girding my loins and stepping through the door.

'I shall take that as a compliment. It is a lovely vista. Almost as lovely as the one I have now.'

Of course, I was walking in front of him. I heard him chuckle softly again as I felt every inch of my body flame.

---

[16]Needless to say, all such escapades were entirely the fault of Fitzroy. Well, if not the fault, at least the instigation that led me into such situations *was* always his fault.

With my hair upswept my neck must have given away my embarrassment. 'You really are too charming,' he said.

I should note here that what Otto said could have been said in a mocking or even a smug tone, but it was not. If I had been the kind of women to sneak off with him, and not a spy who was fearful her cover, or worse, would be exposed at any moment, I think I would have liked him. There was no pretence about him. No attempt at seduction. He had offered an adventure and been quite clear about what it would involve. I have no doubt if I had refused, he would have paid for our drinks and said good night, content with the thought that at least his reputation as a rogue would continue. He might even have continued the conversation if I was willing, even if I had not succumbed to his lure. I suspected he genuinely enjoyed the company of women – even when they kept their clothes on.

I reached a door at the top of the small stair and it opened out onto the third landing. 'See, there is nothing to fear,' said Otto. I realised I must have given a sigh of relief.

'I've never done anything like this before,' I said.

'As we have previously established. Believe me, the combination of emotions of fear and excitement is an intoxicating mix. I have no doubt you will enjoy other adventures in your career.' He walked to room 327 and took a key from his pocket. 'I only caution you to be very careful as to whom you select as your partner in crime. Not all are as gentlemanly as I am.'

As he turned his attention to the lock, I put the small bag that held the chloroformed ladies handkerchief behind me and gently pinched the snap lock between my fingers.

It did not budge.

Otto opened the door, placed a guiding hand on my waist and had me through the doorway before I realised it had happened. Of course, in doing so, he had seen me fiddling with bag behind my back. 'Shall I take that for you?' he offered. 'I find it is a good idea to keep all one's possessions together as they are discarded. There is less chance then of anything being forgot.'

'Oh, I wanted to… touch up my lipstick,' I said.

Otto approached me and stood so close I could feel the heat from his body. 'Now is not the time for such trivialities,' he said and removed the bag from my grasp. He reached up his hands and unpinned my shawl. 'I have been wanting to do that since I first saw you.'

I displayed more of myself than I wished, but perhaps I could use this as a distraction? I breathed in, inflating my upper body. To my relief the tight and low décolletage did manage to continue to contain me. His gaze lowered. Finally, I had the upper hand. I reached out a hand to the edge of his lapel and traced the outline with my finger. I spoke in what I hoped sounded like a seductively husky voice and not as if I had suddenly acquired an inflamed throat. 'I want to look perfect for you,' I said. 'Please let me do a little touch-up.' I reached out my other hand to remove the bag from his slackened grasp. My fingers had touched the smooth sides of the reticule when, it transpired, I had done my act too well. Otto threw both shawl and bag behind me and gathered me in his embrace, crushing my arms between us. He then placed his lips to mine and kissed me passionately. I was wholly at his mercy.

My first thought was that I had better never tell Bertram about this. My second was that without the chloroform I would never be able to overpower such a big man. My third was this man intended me no harm. He believed me willing. My fourth was that I had better go with it. I could pretend I was kissing someone else. After all things could go no further without us both removing other items of clothing, some of which, especially on my side, were not without their complexity. Fifth, I decided If Bertram ever found out I would say I was kissing him for my country and blame it squarely on Fitzroy. My final thought, all of these occurring at ridiculous speed as one generally thinks in these sorts of situations, was where the hell was the wretched spy? Then I surrender myself to his embrace and kissed him back. After all, I was pretending to be a married woman.

Mere moments later than I care to admit, we both emerged, a little breathless, from the kiss.

'My dear, if that is a taste of things to come, then tonight I count myself the luckiest man in this kingdom.'

I smiled. 'But now I really must insist on having my bag,' I said. 'I have a number of pins in my hair and I would not wish to leave them scattered across your room.'

He sighed. 'I suppose we must be practical.' He handed me back my bag.

'If you wish,' I said trying my husky voice again, 'You could always take the pins out yourself.'

Again, the lock would not budge. Otto saw me struggling and took it off me. 'Here, let me,' he said. 'New, is it? These fancy catches can be stiff at first.' He pinched the lock and again it did not move. He tried harder, his knuckles whitening with the effort. My heart was in my mouth. What if the handkerchief fell out? I tensed ready to snatch it up. He lifted the bag up to his eye level and tried once again. This time the catch gave and the lip of the reticule swung open. It did so as he had his face close to it. He pulled his head up sharply. 'What the hell is this?' he said. He staggered slightly and dropped the bag and contents. 'What game are you...' His words slurred. I went for the cloth. I could not count he had taken enough to be made more than giddy.

Unfortunately, this assumption proved correct. I reached past him for my weapon only to feel his arms come once more around my waist. Only this time it was no passionate embrace.

Chapter Twelve

I struggled. Of course I did. But I was much, much smaller than Otto. As I tried to break free, he lifted me off my feet.

'What are you about?' he cried. 'Who sent you?'

Midair I fought even harder for my freedom. I tried to twist from side to side, but to no avail. He held me fast.

What happened next came as a surprise to both of us. This uncomfortable embrace, the pressure of his arms against my body, became familiar – and without conscious thought I raised my left foot high and then drove it backwards with all my force against his knee, which gave sickeningly. As an extra measure, for I have always been an attentive student regardless of subject, I threw my head back, making hard contact with Otto's nose

Just before Otto collapsed onto the bed, several sounds occurred at the same time. I believe I made some kind of cry. Otto gave an 'oof' of pain and I heard the crack of his nose breaking. He released me as he fell, and I dropped to the floor.

At this point Fitzroy burst through the door in the most indiscreet manner possible. The door behind him swung loosely on one hinge. I barely noticed this. On all fours I reached to snatch the handkerchief and finish the job.

Yet again I failed to retrieve the accursed cloth. This time it was Fitzroy who caught hold of me, half-lifting, half-carrying me over to a chair. As I sat, I saw his face had gone white as a sheet.

'The door,' I said, 'someone will see.'

'Bugger the door,' he said, reaching up a hand behind my head and peering into my eyes. 'How badly are you hurt?' He brought his hand back wet with blood. I looked at it blankly for a moment.

'Alice, where does it hurt?' he said urgently.

I blinked. 'That's not mine. I think I broke his nose.' Only at this point did I realise Fitzroy had paid no attention to Otto. He had been solely focused on me.

'I am well,' I said. 'My head is a trifle sore and I may have a bruise, but nothing more. The door?'

Fitzroy swore again, rather more crudely[17] and went to prop the door back into the frame. 'That will have to do,' he said, marching over to Otto. He leant over the bed, checking the fallen man. 'Well, I'm happy to say you haven't killed him.'

'I only did what you showed me,' I said in a rather small voice.

'Right. We'd better roll him up in the bedspread. With luck the blood hasn't seeped through yet to the sheets. I'd suggest stuffing a pillow over his nose to stop him dripping, but that really would finish what you've started.'

'Did I do something wrong?' I asked standing up.

Fitzroy looked up at me. I watched as the tense expression faded from his face. 'I am presuming you improvised after some mishap?'

'The clasp would not open... he offered to open it...' I didn't get much further. The room tilted to a strange angle and I sat back down again quickly. Light danced in front of my eyes and I felt rather queer.

---

[17]Sometimes I did have occasion to wish he acted like a gentleman around me. His knowledge of curse words is extensive and all too explicit.

The next thing I knew there was a dreadful smell under my nose. Fitzroy recorked a bottle of smelling salts. 'No time for fainting, Alice. We have to get him out of here and downstairs. Wait a moment.' I sat there attempting to coalesce my thoughts. Get Otto downstairs? How? Why? Why had I never asked what we were going to do with the man?

Fitzroy reappeared with a damp towel. 'Lean forward. I have to get this blood off you.' Under his efforts the towel turned a violent shade of red. 'Sit there, while I wrap him up.'

He bundled Otto up in the counterpane, tucking the towel in with him, but not over his face. Once he had the bundle as neat as he wished, he stepped back and looked at me appraisingly. 'You'll need to hold the door open for me when I come back.' With that he left. I picked up the bag and handkerchief and put one inside the other. 'Now,' came an urgent voice at the door. I opened it and Fitzroy wheeled in a large wicker basket. 'Stroke of luck I found this,' he said. 'I thought you and I were going to have to lug him down the back stairs. And you're in no state to do that. Help me lift him in. Take the feet. No, the other end.'

We got him into the laundry basket in what, under other circumstances, would have been a farcical manner. 'It's easy to push,' said Fitzroy. 'I'll go first and wave you on if the way is clear. There's a staff elevator not too far away. If fortune favours us, we'll brush thought this all right.'

'What about the door?' I said.

'Will you forget the bloody door?' said Fitzroy. 'It'll lend credence to the idea he's been abducted.'

'We are abducting him,' I pointed out.

'No, we're not,' said Fitzroy. 'We're not criminals. We are agents of the Crown and we do not commit criminal acts.

Now come on.'

Between us we navigated the corridor, got into the lift and back down to our own floor. The whole experience was extremely nerve-wracking, but we managed to avoid all other living souls. Finally, we wheeled the basket into our room.

'What now?' I asked.

'Open the window. He should be waiting.'

I heaved up the sash to see a motor car drawn up tight to the wall. 'Hi-ho,' said a chipper, fresh-faced young man. 'How jolly, a girl. I believe you have a delivery for me.'

Fitzroy wheeled the hamper over and between us we hoisted Otto through the window. I could feel laughter bubbling up inside me. I had to bite my lip to prevent myself from dissolving into hysterics. The receiving young gentleman struggled manfully with the package and wrestled it onto his backseat where he threw a rug over it. 'How long will he be out, do you think?' he asked Fitzroy.

'Ask her. She knocked him out.'

'Golly gosh,' said the driver. 'Nice bit of work. I'd better tootle. Never can tell with a concussion how long it's liable to last.' And with that he hopped into the driving seat and drove off. I half expected him to sound his horn in farewell and wave goodbye to us, perhaps issuing an invitation to a game of tennis or tea over his shoulder as he left, but he did not.

I sat down in another of the hotel's comfortable chairs. Fitzroy pulled my shawl out of the laundry hamper and passed it to me. 'You should pin that back on before you catch your death,' he said. 'I'll be back in a moment when I've got rid of this thing.'

When he had gone, I took a look at myself in the mirror and once again came near to fainting. No wonder the young man in the car had looked so delighted to see me. I hoisted up my dress, and by the time Fitzroy returned, I had my shawl pinned tightly on.

'I preferred it the other way.'

'You are outrageous,' I said.

'You forgot to pick up your shawl, which could have caused us both a lot of trouble.'

'You were late,' I countered.

'I was not,' said Fitzroy, indignation sounding in his voice. 'How was I to know you could seduce a stranger with such alacrity? You were faster than a lot of pros!'

'Professional spies?'

'No, pros.'

'You mean prostit...' I picked up a glass from the dressing table and threw it at him. It smashed against the wall. Fitzroy didn't even blink.

'Missed by a mile, Alice. Your aim is lousy,' said the spy. 'We'll have to work on that.'

'You...' I stalked towards him. Fitzroy held up his hands in surrender.

'Pax. We got the job done. We can talk it over later. I, for one, want a whisky.' He poured himself one and passed another to me. 'God knows, I don't know when I've taken part in such a ridiculous set of circumstances. I hope it isn't always going to be like this with you. I'm not sure I could take it.'

I ignored this. 'Why did you want him? Am I allowed to know?'

'Damned if I know,' said the spy swigging from his glass. 'Told you it wasn't my operation. I was simply helping after another couple had to bow out.'

For the first time in my life I felt my jaw drop open.

The corners of Fitzroy's lips twitched. 'I know I always

come across enigmatic and omniscient, Alice, but the truth –
and I'm sorry to break this to you – but the truth is I don't
always know what it is going on, or why it is going on.'

'You don't know…' I said slowly. 'You don't know…'
This was the last straw. I could no longer contain myself and
broke into laughter. Fitzroy raised his eyebrows, but it
wasn't long before he joined me in my mirth.

'I'll give you this, Alice, I laugh more when you're
around.'

'Drink up. We have to go down to dinner.'

'After this?' I said. All humour draining out of my soul.

'Especially after this. We need to sit down and have a
nice supper with all the other nice people here. We have to
show we are as nice as the rest. You may confine yourself to
womanly trifles. If you get a headache or feel dizzy come
over a little tipsy and I'll take you upstairs.'

'I am already both,' I said. 'My head hurts like billy-o
and I've already had two whiskies and a glass of
champagne.' I looked at his accusingly. 'Did you know the
tea here has sandwiches and cakes so small you can barely
see them on the plate.'

'Oh Lord,' said Fitzroy. He went into the en suite and
returned with another towel.

'Do I still have blood in my hair?'

'No, you are more than halfway to being drunk.' He
placed the towel, which he had managed to get icy cold,
across the back of my neck. I would have jumped out of my
seat, but he had one heavy hand on my shoulder. So instead I
uttered a cry of protest. I immediately felt nauseous.
Fortunately, this passed without incident. My fuzziness of
mind cleared to a remarkable degree. 'Unpleasant, I know,'
said Fitzroy, 'but it does the job. No more alcohol for you

tonight.'

'I have no problem with that,' I said. 'I do not even like the stuff.'

'Thank goodness for that. If you did, I imagine you would be three sheets to the wind by now.'

Dinner proved to be as dull as Fitzroy had suggested. He paid scandalous attention to the woman seated on the other side of me and ignored me. The gentleman to my right did the same. I sated my hunger and curbed my desire to kick the spy in the shins. After dinner Fitzroy got us a small table in the centre of the bar and left me there with a glass of lemonade. He moved about the room chatting to various men, looking over at me occasionally to ensure I was still in my designated place. I kept my eyes mostly lowered. It felt as if all eyes were on me. After what seemed and age, he appeared at my side and offered me his arm. 'Time for bed, Alice.'

I rose and walked with him out into the lobby. At this point I presumed we would be making a quick exit to the car, but instead he walked us off smartly to our room. He opened the door and ushered me in. I felt despite my initial impression, I could quickly come to hate hotels. Men seemed to usher me about a lot in them and I did not like it.

He locked the door behind us. 'Don't worry,' he said. 'I'll take the floor or maybe the bath. You can have the bed.'

'We're staying?' I said. 'In the same room?'

'The world thinks us married.'

'But…'

'Don't worry, Alice. I regard our relationship as purely professional.'

'Was it professionalism that made you pay so much attention to that blonde at dinner?'

Fitzroy cocked his head on one side and gave me a funny

look. 'I was doing my best to ensure everyone saw where we were meant to be this evening, so that when they discover the kidnapping tomorrow no one will think of questioning us.'

'Oh,' I said.

'Besides, we are meant to married, and from my observation, that generally seems to stymie the conversation.'

'Do we at least get to stay for breakfast?' I said.

'Such interest in food. I fear you have been overly affected by Richenda. Yes, Alice, we get to stay for breakfast. It would look too odd if we didn't. I suggest you pretend to have a headache from overindulgence. I told several people how I had had to tell the barman to stop serving you.'

I gave him a pained look.

'All in the name of the Crown, of course.'

I sighed. 'I won't have to act. My head is still throbbing.'

Fitzroy reached into his pocket and pulled out a clean handkerchief. He unfolded it and revealed two tablets. 'Painkillers,' he said. 'I thought you might need them.'

'Thank you,' I said and washed them down with the remnants of the whisky I had left in the room earlier. Fitzroy opened his mouth to say something then seemed to change his mind. 'Get into bed, Alice. I'll sleep in the bath. Don't snore.'

I was too tired to respond to this quip. Moments after he closed the bathroom door, I threw off my clothes, not caring if I tore them in the process, and climbed between the sheets. Within moments of my head touching the pillow I was asleep.

Chapter Thirteen

I awoke to see Fitzroy, fully dressed, sitting in a chair, studying the notebook I had found in the Mullers' church. He looked up. 'Good morning.'

'Oh no, have I missed breakfast?'

Fitzroy grinned. 'Such interest in food again. No, you have not. There is plenty of time for us to go down. It's early. I don't tend to sleep much.'

I looked pointedly at him.

'I'm studying your book, not looking at you. Besides, I've seen a lady in her night attire before.'

'I am not wearing any,' I said, tugging the sheet up tightly.

Fitzroy looked up at me and raised an eyebrow. 'Really, Alice, you must try not to tumble into bed drunk all the time.'

'You kept giving me whisky!'

He ignored my comment and waved the book at me. 'This is rather fun. I thought I'd got it twice, but more and more I'm beginning to think the wretched thing needs a key. By which I mean a name or a phrase.'

'I presume you have considered all the obvious ones,' I said in an attempt to speak with some authority in my undressed situation.

'I think we can presume even Richard would not be so stupid. But, yes, I did try a few. You never know when fortune will favour you. I never thought Richard the brainy type, but he could be cunning.'

'It is a shame we never found Mrs Wilson's diary.'

Fitzroy regarded me blankly for a moment. 'Oh, yes. Sorry. I have to remember a lot of things.'

'Perhaps you could go down to breakfast before me?'

'That's what I intend. However, I suspect we will have to give statements to the police. I rather hope they notice he is missing before we leave. Get that out of the way and then we need to be off.'

I nodded my assent to the plan. He didn't move. But stared thoughtfully at the wall above my head.

'Is there anything else?' I said eventually.

'What? Oh yes, could you give me a brief summary of what happened between you and old Otto last night? By brief I mean succinct, not missing out details.'

I managed to wiggle a pillow behind my back and pull up the counterpane, so I was facing him better. I then began my tale. As much as possible, I attempted to repeat what we had said verbatim. I got a nod of approval at the way I handled Otto at the bar. However, the conversation on the landing made him frown. When I mentioned the secret stairs, I thought I heard a muted 'Oh God', but I couldn't be sure. But when I started to explain what had happened in the room before he arrived the 'Oh Gods' became louder and more frequent. His head sunk lower and lower, so that by the time I had finished it was in his hands. I stopped and waited for him to respond.

Fitzroy gave a heavy sigh and raised his head. 'Do you, by any chance, have any idea of what you did wrong? Or even how much danger you were placing yourself in? Did you recognise any of the warnings?'

'I thought the secret stairs was a bit risky,' I admitted. 'But I couldn't think of a way out of that. And then in the room just before he kissed me… it all got a bit difficult.'

'A bit difficult,' said Fitzroy from under a heavy frown. I

125

inched down in the bed slightly. His expression could best be described as thunderous. 'A bit difficult!' His voice rose in volume – although I noticed he took care to keep it a level that would defy an eavesdropper. 'You tried to seduce the man!'

'You asked me to do so!'

'I asked you to get him to his room and chloroform him. I said nothing about using husky voices and removing hair pins or articles of clothing. Good God, girl, if Otto hadn't been a gentleman at heart, I dread to think what would have happened.'

'I was improvising,' I said. I knew my voice sounded angry and rude, but it was either that or burst into tears.

'And as for kissing him passionately!'

'By that time what choice did I have?'

'I might as well have employed a prostitute. She would have been to handle things far more smoothly. If I had known you were willing to take off your clothes, I could have given far simpler instructions. It is much easier to chloroform a man after he has had sex.'

I sat bolt upright, clutching the sheet to my front. 'That is too harsh,' I said. 'I never had any intention…'

Fitzroy held up his hand cutting me off. 'Yes, it was harsh. Probably too harsh, but honestly, Euphemia, I thought you were more self-aware of the effect you have on men? You explained it to me quite clearly before. If you had been fully trained in martial defence, I might have countenanced what you had done, but you were extremely lucky he caught and held you as he did. Many men would have held you down and ravished you.'

'You do not think much of your sex,' I said sternly, but I could feel myself trembling.

'When they are with a half-naked woman, who willingly

went into their bedchamber? No, I don't.'

'I wonder you sent me at all.'

'I happen to know that Otto von Wolff is at heart a decent fellow, or I wouldn't have sent you. *But you did not know that.* I am frustrated and angry... do you know what causes the death of the majority of spies, regardless of who they are working for?'

I shook my head not trusting myself to speak.

'Over-confidence,' said Fitzroy. He stood up and tucked the pocket book into the inside of his jacket. 'I am going down to breakfast. Join me as soon as you can. You don't need to pack up the clothes neatly but do put them in the cases. It would look odd if we left any behind.' He walked to the door. 'When I see you downstairs, I will be your husband, Mr Brown. As for what happened here yesterday will discuss that at another time when I have the space and patience to explain what you did wrong. Perhaps in the meantime you can think about that for yourself?' He left, closing the door behind him.

By the time I had dressed, fixed my hair, and packed, the gentleman I met downstairs could not have been more charming. My husband held out my seat for me, chided me gently on my drinking last night, and apologised once more for running over our imaginary cat. He then started to discuss what school we might send Nicolas to. He told me he agreed to a local prep as I had requested, as long as his education was finished somewhere decent – which he then went on to discuss at tiresome length. Not only had his manner changed, but his mannerisms too. Mr Brown had a habit of stroking his moustache when he was thinking and drumming his fingers on the tablecloth. He also ate with an almost finicky precision, totally unlike Fitzroy. I realised I was watching the performance of a master. He did not need different clothing to shift into an entirely different persona. I forgot about our disagreement and watched fascinated. I made a plethora of mental notes.

A policeman joined as we were finishing our morning tea. Mr Brown preferred his wife give her statement in his presence unless the constable could think of a reason why she should not? Not being under any obvious suspicion he came across as a most controlling husband, who did not like letting his wife out of his sight. Another mark against us being involved with Otto. We both gave simple statements. Fitzroy gave a fictitious forwarding address. He then paid the hotel bill, keeping me by his side, got the porters to bring down the luggage and load it into the car. Then, almost before I realised, we were driving away.

'I am glad you had the sense to keep that choker,' said Fitzroy after a couple of miles. We'll dump the rest of the stuff, but you can wear that to cover your bruises. I have been thinking about what you said…'

I must have looked cowed because he added, 'Not that. About Mrs Wilson. I think you might be right. The key might still be somewhere in Stapleford Hall.'

'He had other properties.'

'Agreed, but that was his favourite, was it not?'

'He was obsessed with the place,' I said.

'We need to think of a way to get you in there. Who lives there now?'

'I don't know. Bertram took no interest in the place and Hans drew up a document exempting him and Richenda from inheriting it.'

'Hmm, but presumably it would have had a codicil about who it went to in the case Richard predeceased the rest of his family without an heir?'

'It was never discussed with me, or in front of me,' I said.

'Nevertheless it's the kind of clause lawyers live for. Any idea when the will shall be read? Or has it already been done?'

'I think both Bertram and Richenda thought he would leave everything to his wife.'

'Lucinda, was it? Daughter of a mill owner?'

'I believe her dowry consisted of a number of mills.'

'And who will they go to now know he's gone?' He gave a grimace of disgust. 'I do hope this doesn't turn out to be a grubby little matter about inheritance. That is the kind of the thing the ordinary police should have been able to easily solve.'

'You are involved because you believe the circumstances of his death have some kind of national importance?'

Fitzroy negotiated a tight corner before answering. 'If anything, I would be interested in who gets the armaments factory now – and possibly even the bank. The actual matter of his death matters less to the service than what becomes of his assets, and if we can still utilise them for the security of the country.'

'Oh, I see. A single person's situation is not important enough to affect national security?'

'Not in the usual way of things. Of course, if the King had been involved…'

'Naturally,' I said.

The conversation between us died. It took some time for me to get up the nerve to ask, 'Then why are you involved.'

Fitzroy threw me a startled look, and almost skidded. 'Because of you, of course. I thought I had made that adequately clear.'

'Oh,' I said again.

'That doesn't mean I am not still furious with you. We will have words later. Right now, I have other matters on my

129

mind.'

I took this as a request for my silence. I made no more attempts at conversation and did not even ask where we were headed. I hoped such supplication might have a minor effect on his temper.

Chapter Fourteen

It quickly transpired that I had no need to enquire of our destination. The landscape became familiar. 'You are taking me back to the Mullers.'

'I do wish your friend Hans had listened to me and changed both his names. He sounds far too German.'

'Perhaps he is proud of his German heritage.'

'Then once war is formally declared he will find himself being proud of it in an internment camp along with his wife and children.'

'You cannot be serious?'

'No, changing his name would, in all likelihood, not have been enough. His parentage is too well known. Is that not why he had to resort to seeking business from Richard Stapleford? Less and less of those in the City would work with him.'

'But Hans would never do -'

Fitzroy interrupted me. 'Why not? You are prepared to swear your loyalty to your country, why would he not be prepared to do the same?'

'Because he considers himself an English gentleman,' I said hotly.

Fitzroy slowed the car and pulled in to a sheltered path off the road. 'Are you sure about that? The subterfuge he could be exercising would be no more than I did with my German princess.'

'But you are not German.'

Fitzroy said something in German I could not follow, but the words were fluid and convincing. 'You speak German?'

'I speak a few languages. I have had an odd linguistic aptitude since I was a child. I don't care to use it often.'

'Is that why you said you were good at codes?'

'My point, Euphemia, is that I do not believe the German people are in any way lesser than the English, nor do I find them individually evil. However, when a country becomes our foe then we must treat its subjects like foes. We no longer have the luxury of trusting them, and in a conflict we must often slay them to preserve our own lives. Personally, I consider war a failure on both sides to communicate and reason. Once fighting begins, both sides lose – mothers lose sons and sons lose fathers. The laws of human society change. We are forced to be cruel and callous to defend our country's beliefs – the lot of the ordinary people on both sides is little different. However, having expressed my opinion, which I rarely do, I must make it clear to you that I will show no leniency when I am called to war. I will undertake whatever my sovereign requires of me. If I am told to personally drag Hans into a jail, I will do so. If I am told to investigate him and find him an enemy of the state, then I will consign him to the firing squad. You also, Euphemia, have sworn to do the same.'

I felt bile rise in my throat.

'You cannot say I did not warn you about this work.'

'No,' I said. 'I cannot. But I did not think about how close to me and mine…'

'I hoped you had.'

'Is there nothing that can be done for Hans?' I said. 'What will happen to Richenda and the children? Must they also be interned?'

'I don't know. Her twin's past actions do not argue well for her own. In marrying a German, she has been thought to be playing both sides. She shares the ownership of the

Stapleford Bank, doesn't she? She'd be wise to sign it over to Bertram. It is possible it could be confiscated by the government.'

I began to tremble. 'Dear God, this is awful.'

'I thought it better to raise this before we returned to the estate. If it occurred to you there…'

'You thought I might warn them?'

'Actually no, I didn't think you would go against your oath, but I did thing the realisation of what may be coming to that family would shake you to the core. Better to consider the situation before you are called upon to act as if all is normal.'

'Yes, I see that,' I said quietly. 'You are right. I will hate myself, but I will not warn them. I gave my word.'

'War is an ugly business, Euphemia. If it helps, the work we do is to avoid conflict and if that cannot be accomplished, then it is to seek information that will end the war as quickly as possible – with our victory, of course.'

'That makes it sound like spying is a positive thing.'

Fitzroy frowned. 'Of course, it is. We do what must be done to preserve and shelter the rest of our fellow countrymen.'

'You truly believe that?'

'Why else do you think I would do the things I have done?'

I gave myself a shake. 'Yes, I know. I have expressed the exact same thought to you after…'

'I've done something awful,' finished the spy.

'Yes,' I said. 'I am merely accustoming myself to the idea that I may be called upon do such things.'

'Oh, while I'm training you, I get first dibs on doing that stuff,' said Fitzroy, and I could hear how he was struggling to lighten the mood. He started the engine again.

'So, do I become Euphemia within a certain distance of places I have lived?' I asked trying to match his tone.

He continued looking straight ahead. 'I certainly wouldn't call you Alice in front of your family, but no – this time it was… well, you'll work it out.'

'Because you were speaking to me as a friend?'

'Let's just say it was a conversation that officially never took place.'

I sank back into my thoughts for some time. When we were almost at the estate, the spy finally spoke again, 'Do remember to keep that choker on. I don't want Bertram coming after me with a fire poker or some such thing. You'd hate it if I broke him.'

'Are you coming to the estate with me?'

'I haven't decided. Tonight, I will stop at the village inn. Do tell me they don't have bedbugs? I need to send some messages. I presume there is a local post office?'

'Yes to the post office. I would not know about bedbugs.'

'The charms of the countryside,' said Fitzroy. 'Depending on what telegram I get back I may join you. Otherwise I would like you to come down to the village tomorrow after lunch and we can discuss what we will do next. We need to somehow get access to Stapleford Hall.'

'I hope you will at least drive me up to the house this time. The Chilterns were less than friendly last time.'

'Who?'

'The gatekeepers.'

'Probably didn't want a murderess in their house.'

'Are we being friends or professionals at this moment?'

'Why?'

'Because if we are friends, I am going to hit you.'

'Definitely professionals,' said Fitzroy turning briefly to wink at me.

Stone opened the door to the pair of us. Fitzroy had parked the car and accompanied me up the stairs without explanation. As I expected everyone to be even more angry with me, I did not complain. The Mullers' stoic butler gave an almost inaudible sigh when he saw who was at the door. 'I will announce you, miss, sir. The family are at luncheon. He left us waiting in the hall.

'If I did not know better,' I said quietly to Fitzroy, 'I would think you arranged things to gain maximum access to meals.'

The spy bent down to whisper in my ear. 'How do you know I don't.' I gave a slight laugh and caught sight of my potential fiancé standing watching us from the other side of the hall. 'Bertram,' I said, held out my hands. 'I can explain.'

'I would rather not know,' said my beloved. He nodded at Fitzroy.

'Good to see you, Stapleford. I know I'm meant to say I'm sorry for your loss, but I'm not and I doubt you are either.'

I could see Bertram struggling not to smile. 'I am containing my sorrow tolerably,' he said.

'Contenting yourself with remembering him as a sweet little boy with whom you played adorable japes?' said Fitzroy.

'No,' said Bertram. 'He was born a bastard.' He blushed. 'Well, not literally, but you know what I mean.'

'So, you two lovebirds are not going to quarrel?' said Fitzroy. 'Euphemia was rather scared of confronting you on her own.'

'I would infinitely prefer it if you would stop running off with my fiancée,' said Bertram. 'It is most difficult to explain, let alone personally aggrieving.'

'I assure you, on my word,' said Fitzroy, 'it has all been entirely professional. In fact, I'm going to need to talk to her again later on this afternoon.'

'What about?'

'I won't know that until later,' said the spy. 'So I can't tell you.'

Bertram sighed heavily. 'Whatever. You'd better come and have some lunch, Euphemia. Your mother and Joe are still here, but I warn you, Richenda's gone off. It's all a bit sombre.'

'Gone off?'

'Even taken the children,' said Bertram.

I became acutely aware of Fitzroy listening intently beside me. 'Where?' I asked.

'You won't believe it, she's -' said Bertram.

'Stapleford Hall,' I interrupted.

'You knew!'

'I assure you, neither Euphemia or myself knew. We have been busy elsewhere.'

'How is Hans taking it?' I asked.

'Badly,' said Bertram.

'On that note, I think I will take my leave,' said Fitzroy. 'I was going to invite myself to luncheon despite Euphemia's mother being present, which should tell you how hungry I am. But I draw the line at moping husbands.' And without further farewell he let himself out of the house, mortally offending Stone, who believed almost religiously that the front door should never come into contact with any hand other than his own.

'The smoked salmon is rather good,' said Bertram, taking my hand and leading me into the dining room. 'And there's some fishy-tasting sandwiches which are much better than they sound. Joe thinks there is Apple Charlotte for sweet, but

I think he's dreaming.'

'It sounds a very odd meal,' I said as we entered.

'Well, Richenda going off like that rather threw the household out of whack.' He said this as we stood on the threshold of the room, a mite too loudly, as Hans looked up from his seat at the head of the table.

'In reality, Bertram, the only person who ever ran this household properly was Euphemia,' he said calmly. 'You have made an excellent choice in a wife. Unlike, it would appear, myself.'

'Yes, well, oh, um...' said Bertram holding out a chair.

'Euphemia, how nice of you to drop by and see us again,' said my mother. 'Where exactly are you residing now?'

Joe grinned at me from the other side of the table. He was not yet too old to delight in his older sister being berated by his mother. It was generally he that was in trouble.

'Indeed, Mother,' I said sitting down, 'I have been taken around the country so much, I am not sure myself. It appears when one is accused of a crime one did not commit there is a great deal of paperwork to do to ensure various people do not try and re-arrest one.'

'Poppycock,' said my mother. I almost spilled my glass in shock. 'But if you won't tell me of your own accord,' she continued. 'I am certainly not going to beg. Bertram, I hope you know what you are doing marrying this girl – and I hope even more fervently that once married you will bring her to heel.'

'Mother!' I said, appalled. Joe stuffed his napkin in his mouth to smother his giggles. Even Hans gave a slight, sad smile.

Bertram became very interested in a speck of dust on his shoes and almost disappeared under the table.

I helped myself to some salmon and some fresh green

beans. I had a great many questions I wished to ask but launching into them at once would appear far too odd. Instead I let my mother rattle on chastising me for a while. I thought that of all the people present, she was the one I had most pleased by giving her cause to scold me. Although, doubtless, Joe was glad to have the maternal spotlight for once turned away from him.

When she paused for breath, Hans said, 'I suppose it would be too much to hope that Richenda communicated her intentions to you, Euphemia?'

'I am sorry, Hans, but she did not. When I learned where she had gone, I was shocked.' Bertram gave me a funny look. He opened his mouth to say, presumably, that I had guessed far too easily, but I kicked him heavily on the shin under the table. So instead of speaking he gave an 'ouch' of pain. Then he gave me the broadest smile. I knew he did not relish the bruise, but my action had reminded him of the many times we had worked together for the Crown. He had finally tumbled to the fact that I was truly working with Fitzroy again. Bertram looked at me in the soppiest way. I smiled back inwardly wondering what the spy would say when he discovered Bertram knew I was working with him again. But then, no one could accuse me of telling him.

Luncheon dragged on to its inevitable conclusion. There was no Apple Charlotte, but a Bakewell tart sated Joe. We had barely left the room when Bertram dragged me off for a walk around the garden.

'So, are you working on Richard's murder with old Fizz-bang or is it something juicer? And why did he not include me?' he said as soon as we were a reasonable distance from the house.

'Old Fizz-bang?' I said, struggling to contain my mirth. 'I must tell him that.'

Bertram immediately looked alarmed. 'I would much rather you did not,' he said.

'Never mind that,' I said. 'To be honest, he has involved me in a number of things, and I do not have any idea of how they all add together. I suspect he is working on more than one problem at once. Besides, you know how communicative he generally is.'

'Has he shot anyone this time?'

'Not yet,' I said. 'But then it has only been a couple of days.' I intended the comment to be light-hearted, but Bertram's face darkened.

'I know I have no right now, or ever, to control your actions,' he said, 'but that man takes you to some dark places. It has got to have some effect on your soul.'

'I assure you, I am the same as I ever was,' I said, smiling up at him.

'No, you are not,' said Bertram. 'You are so far different from the maid I met hunting for books in my bed that I barely recognise you.'

'Indeed, I have changed,' I said earnestly.

'I did not say all the changes were for the worse,' said Bertram. By now we had reached the lodge gates.

'Where are we going?'

'Fitzroy said you were to come to the village to meet him after luncheon, did he not?'

'Yes.'

'Well, if you think I am giving that cad the opportunity to spirit you away again without so much as a farewell, he – and you – can damn well think again. Whatever is going on, I am involved now – and he will have to lump it.' He set his face into a mulish expression and quickened his pace.

'Bertram,' I said gently. 'I do not think this is a good idea.'

'I can walk in front of you or behind,' said my fiancé, 'but you are not abandoning me again to the Mullers' marital woes and your damn mother. I don't mean to be rude about your family, Euphemia, but one minute the wretched woman is looking at me like I'm a poor lost lamb about to go off to the butcher's and the next she's telling me to man up and fetch you back myself. As if I could when I had no idea where in England you had gone.'

'It must have been most unpleasant,' I said, doing my best to avoid answering any questions. I knew I was going to have to contend with Fitzroy's reaction to what Bertram knew so far, let alone his presence. I was not looking forward to either.

We found the little inn quite easily. Apparently, it was not uncommon for Hans and Bertram to slope off here after their evening's game of billiards. The innkeeper, who at least kept a ladies' salon, asked if I was looking for Mr Brown and when I assented, said he had been told to tell me to wait and that my husband would be back momentarily.

'Your husband!' growled Bertram, when the man had gone back to the main bar. 'Should I be asking exactly what is going on?'

At this moment the adjoining door to the bar from the salon opened and Fitzroy walked in. He took one look at Bertram and then turned his furious expression in my direction. 'What the hell is he doing here?' he demanded.

Chapter Fifteen

'Bertram was concerned for my wellbeing with that tramp – the one who killed Richard – still being on the loose. He was determined to accompany me,' I said.

Fitzroy scowled more deeply.

'There's no need to look like that, man,' said Bertram. 'I would have thought in your profession you were more than aware of the dangers inherent in our modern world. Can't leave young women unprotected, can we?'

Fitzroy made a soft sound somewhere between a growl and a snarl. 'Besides,' continued Bertram, apparently oblivious to the spy's worsening mood, 'I'd think after all you've been doing to clear *my fiancée's* name, you would have a vested interest in keeping her safe.'

The two men exchanged looks that I could not follow.[18]

'I didn't tell him anything, Fitzroy. He guessed when I stood on his foot and kicked him in the shin.'

This caught the spy's attention. 'That sounds like a most unlikely form of communication.'

Bertram gave me another soppy smile. 'Quite romantic actually. She's always done that when she thinks I am about to put my foot in it. Even said she'd buy me a pair of steel toe-capped boots as a wedding present as she had no doubt it was a skill she'd need to continue to use on me throughout our marriage.' He paused a moment. 'I say, Euphemia…'

'Yes, I did buy them for you,' I said with a sigh. 'They

---

[18]Sometimes I fear for the sensible half of the human race – by which I mean, of course, the females.

are wrapped up under my bed back at the house.'

'Oh,' said Bertram, utilising both a soppy smile and brimming tears of affection.

'Good grief,' said Fitzroy. 'I have no time for these romantic shenanigans.'

'I'm relieved to hear it,' said Bertram.

Fitzroy ignored him and spoke over his head to me. 'I presume Richenda would not think it untoward of you to turn up at Stapleford Hall to check on her wellbeing?'

'She might think Hans had sent me?'

'Might not be a bad idea if it would get her out of the way,' said Fitzroy. 'I'd rather the place was empty. You could talk her into going home.'

'I suppose I might be able to,' I said. Bertram kept opening and shutting his mouth rather like a trout trying for flies. I presumed he wanted to say something, but I felt Fitzroy's attention was better kept from him and I gave no pause to let him enter the conversation. The spy simply ignored him as if he were of no more importance than a chair.[19] 'I do honestly believe she would be better off with Hans. I've learnt more about him than I have liked of late, but on the whole I think he must remain in the category of better than most husbands. Wouldn't you think?'

'Don't ask me,' said Fitzroy. 'I never set the bar high where my own gender is concerned. But yes, considering other matters we previously discussed, we had better head to the Hall. We can even take Bertram with us if you want. It adds more realism to the exploit.'

'Did you get your -'

Fitzroy held up a hand to cut me off. 'Not here and now.'

I nodded my understanding. 'We will head back to the

---

[19]Which must have been rather galling.

estate and gather our things.'

'Give me a moment. I'll settle my bill and drive you up.' He looked closely at Bertram and narrowed his eyes. 'I am loath to leave you alone with anyone who may take advantage of your better nature.'

'Well if that's not the pot calling the kettle black!' cried Bertram, finally breaking into the dialogue.

'I know you,' said the spy. 'You will try to worm secrets out of her based on Euphemia's affection for you. Well, I won't have it. I shall keep you both under my eye.' He gave a sudden flash of a smile. 'In fact, that's why I'm with you. I was the only person on hand available to chaperon you and Bertram. Especially since, as far as Richenda is concerned, I am becoming quite a friend of the family.'

'Bah!' said Bertram in disgust.

I was torn between indignation at Fitzroy's opinion of my ability to keep secrets and humour at Bertram's outrage.[20]

The spy stalked out with a curt command for us to wait. As soon as he was gone Bertram said, 'Come on, Euphemia, let's leg it. I'm fed up with that bloody man getting one up on me. It's my turn.'

'He has a car, Bertram. He would catch us. And I can't promise he wouldn't use some kind of rope to pull us in.'

'Dear God. Has he used you so roughly?'

I smiled. 'No, he has treated me well and behaved like a perfect gentleman towards me. He only misbehaves when there are others around. He does have his reputation as a bit of a cad to consider.' I laughed. 'He's really rather sweet when he is merely being himself.'

'Oh, he is, is he?' said Bertram, his voice roaring like gathering thunder.

---

[20]I did love Bertram so very much.

Fitzroy walked back into the lobby carrying his driving gloves and wearing his long coat. He had his goggles perched high on his head and looked every bit the modern driver. The image suited him, and I was fairly convinced he knew that.

'She says you are sweet,' said Bertram.

Fitzroy stopped as if poleaxed. 'How unutterably nauseating!' he said. 'How dare you, Alice! That's a foul calumny. I could sue.'

'I did find it a bit over the top,' said Bertram. 'I managed to swallow it gentlemanly, but…'

Fitzroy lowered his eyebrows and scowled ferociously at me. This did not have the intended reaction as I giggled. 'Car's been brought round to the front,' snapped Fitzroy and walked out.

'Now you have offended him,' I said.

'Yours words, not mine, rattled him.'

Outside Fitzroy sat in the driver's seat fiddling with something technical to do with the car. 'I say,' said Bertram. 'This is a bit of all right.' He made to give me a hand into the back.

'She sits up front,' said Fitzroy curtly.

Bertram's good humour faded, and his expression became somewhat doleful as he helped me into the passenger seat. 'This is a bit rough,' he muttered. 'I doubt Euphemia even knows what kind of a motor this is.' He scrambled into the back and Fitzroy drove off without another word.

Over the noise of the engine the spy said quietly to me, 'Did you call me sweet?'

'I didn't mean it. I was reassuring him that he neither need worry about your intentions nor your actions towards me. Most husbands-to-be would take great exception to their wife continually running off with another man.'

'I do get that,' said Fitzroy to my surprise. 'He's a good man and he trusts you. However, need I caution you not to tell him what we have been doing?'

'Of course not! I have not said a word. He's guessed it's to do with Richard's killer but nothing else. I even said you had me doing so many things I had no idea how it all tied together. Which, incidentally, is true. I wouldn't have said a word about our working together if I hadn't been put the position of outright lying to him. He knows me far too well and would have seen through my ruse. I decided that would be worse.'

'I thought something of the sort must have happened. I didn't think you were the kind to break your word or I'd have never accepted your oath. But you must see that I have to at least pretend to be vexed about all this? It will make Bertram feel he has the upper hand.'

'I didn't know you cared about his feelings.'

'Whether I might or might not is beside the issue. I don't want Bertram trying to get up his own investigation or led you into some hare-brained scheme. We are almost at the end of the road and I don't want us to be derailed now.'

'Shouldn't it be end of the track in that case?' I said.

'Don't be obtuse, Alice. Or I'll let it slip about you kissing dark strangers.'

'You wouldn't!' I said aghast.

'My dear Alice, you better than most should know I will do whatever it takes to complete the mission.'

'But what is this mission. I didn't ...'

'You don't need to know,' said Fitzroy.

'He calls you Fizz-bang,' I said.

'What?' said Fitzroy almost losing control of the vehicle and incurring a cry of surprise from the back seat.

'My fiancé's nickname for you is Fizz-bang.'

145

'I've a mind to take the next bend so fast the bugger falls out,' growled the spy. 'The disrespect!' With this he lapsed into sulking silence until we reached the Muller estate.

We had barely sighted the house before we saw Hans running down the steps to greet us. Fitzroy turned off the engine. 'Do you have him with you?' said Hans urgently.

'I'm in the back,' spoke up Bertram.

'Not you,' snapped Hans. 'Stone.'

'Your butler?' said Fitzroy. 'I am not in the habit of purloining the servants of others.'

Hans spat out several words in a language I didn't know. Beside me the spy tensed. 'I do not know what has occurred,' he said. 'But I strongly doubt it warrants such language.'

'I did not realise you spoke German,' said Hans. 'I apologise profoundly. I am distressed as my butler is missing.'

'Stone?' said Bertram. 'But he is like the bricks and mortar of this place. Never even heard of the man taking a holiday.'

'He has been overtaken by man's eternal temptation. He has gone to Stapleford Hall. He left me a resignation letter.'

Bertram's jaw dropped and his eyes opened wide. 'He has gone off with my sister?'

'I fear so,' said Hans, casting his eyes down and shaking his head. 'I cannot believe he would desert me thus.'

I looked askance at Fitzroy. He appeared outwardly calm with no expression on his face, but I could see his shoulders shaking very slightly as he suppressed his mirth. I immediately wanted to kick him in the shin or step on his foot like I might with Bertram. However, I had the sense to know that while Bertram would never respond in kind, the spy had been trained to counter any attack without thinking.

146

Then the truth dawned on me. 'He means that Stone has gone to be with Glanville,' I said, letting out a sigh of relief.

'Of course,' said Hans. 'What else could I have meant?'

'Indeed,' said Fitzroy, still utilising a bland expression. 'The loss of a butler on the running of a household is a most serious matter.' I sensed he was going to continue to say something even more unfortunate and cut him off.

'Then this will only be of a temporary nature,' I said. 'Richenda knows in her heart of hearts that you have been an excellent husband to her and father to your children. Her current waywardness is rooted only in her own low self-esteem.'

'What do you mean?' asked Hans, frowning.

'When I marry Bertram...'

'Matters are to continue?' asked Hans.

'Of course,' snapped Bertram and I in unison. Fitzroy's shoulders shook even more. Despite everything, he was enjoying this situation immensely.

'As I was saying, when I marry Bertram, Richenda will need to step up and run this house herself. She has never been trained toward that, as I was. At Stapleford Hall she retains an excellent housekeeper, who requires the minimum of overseeing. Here at your estate she will have much to do. She does not wish to make herself look foolish, especially in front of you. She knows she cannot match your first wife in your affection and that she is very much lesser in beauty than your mistresses.'

'I say, Euphemia!' said Bertram.

---

[21] I nonetheless believed he would genuinely apologise for any aggression against me, as he had done once before at Crystal Palace when I had ended up winded, on the floor, and beneath him with my arm locked in a most uncomfortable position.

'The unvarnished truth can expedite matters,' said Fitzroy. 'But I agree, it would have been more ladylike to allude to some of this.' My toes twitched to kick him, but I concentrated my attention on Hans to see how he would react to my words.

He had looked up, and his previously dull eyes were now alight with hope. 'Do you really think so, Euphemia?'

'How the devil would she know?' said Bertram. 'You never introduced her to one of 'em, did you?'

Fitzroy then sustained a mild coughing fit.

'He means about Richenda being scared,' I said.

'Never scared of anything in all her life!' said Bertram.

'This is the first time she has faced real loss – not just of her twin, but she fears to lose Hans' regard.'

Hans put out a hand and clutched my arm. 'Would you speak with her Euphemia? She would shut the door in my face, but she would listen to you. I will employ a skilled housekeeper if it would make her happy. I will procure any and all servants she requires.'

'You'd be much better sending her to my mother,' I said.

'She's still here,' said Hans.

'Well, there is no one who knows more about running a house than my mother. She was trained from childhood to run a great house – and no doubt would have done if she had not married my father.'

'Euphemia, you are brilliant,' said Hans kissing me on both cheeks, oblivious to the fact both the other gentleman behind me came within an inch of punching him for doing so. He stepped back. 'Will you go to Stapleford Hall and bring her home?' He glanced past me. 'And you, Bertram? Surely she would listen to her brother?'

'I don't see why,' began Bertram, but Fitzroy shifted his weight to one side and stepped on Bertram's foot. 'Ouch!'

148

said my poor beleaguered fiancée.

'Hans, you forget,' I said. 'We are yet to be married. My mother would never approve of such a trip without a chaperon.'

'Could she go too?'

I pretended to think about it, sighing and frowning. 'I do not think she would want to interfere. Besides, we could hardly take Joe with us. He would be very distracting, and frankly, I would fear for your glass houses should we leave him here without my mother's supervision.'

Hans, who was very fond of peaches, paled. 'I could go?'

I shook my head again. 'Should Richenda decide she has made a great mistake and rush back here – and then find you away? I doubt she would even spare the breath to ask why.'

Fitzroy coughed slightly. 'If you will allow me,' he said. 'I could function as a chaperon. You are aware of my bona fides and could have no concerns.'

Hans, who had no clue what Fitzroy did, other than he was vaguely connected to the police, said, 'That would be very kind of you. Inspector?'

'Fitzroy.'

'But I could not possible ask you to intervene in a private family matter,' finished Hans.

'Oh, let him do it,' said Bertram in an exasperated tone. 'I do not think I can bear any more of this infernal chatter.' With this he attempted to storm up the stairs and into the house. Except, he now had a slight limp.

'It appears the matter is settled,' said Fitzroy lightly. He offered me his arm, waiting only for Hans to take the lead back into the house.

'That was unkind,' I said softly to him. 'You have made him limp. I have never done that.'

'You have smaller feet,' responded the spy. 'Besides, I

concur with Bertram, it was getting tedious.'

We entered the hall. Hans disappeared off to apprise my mother of my return. 'I shall break it to her with great charm,' he said without modesty. 'We need to have her support with this plan.'

When he had gone, I faced my mentor. 'You spent most of the conversation trying not to laugh. I saw your shoulders shake.'

Fitzroy gave me a wry smile, 'In small doses I find ordinary people entertaining. Your family especially so. That Bertram would be aghast at the idea of his sister running off with a butler – or even mistaken enough to imagine so - is for me light relief against many of the things we must face. Besides, all that we do is to ensure that ordinary people can have their very ordinary and ridiculous squabbles. Without us, the fiction of their world would be exposed and they would see the real horrors of this world.'

'How philosophical you are today,' I said, but he had shaken me. I knew far more about the world than when I had first entered service, and much of it would have been unthinkable, in the worst way, to my younger self. Now I had given my service to the Crown I could only imagine that the things I would see and do would increase in unpleasantness.

Fitzroy stood watching me. 'Yes,' he said. 'You will see things you will never be able to tell your friends and family about, because they simply would not be able to conceive of the – shall we say – impropriety?'

'You mean as opposed to evil?'

Fitzroy shrugged. 'There is only one way not to be afraid of the dark and that is to be the scariest thing in it.'

I could take no more of this conversation. I went upstairs to gather my things. Then I knocked on Bertram's door. I found him sitting on the edge of his bed with one shoe off, massaging his foot. 'That man is a rotter,' he said vehemently.

At that moment I agreed wholeheartedly with him.

Chapter Sixteen

I bade my mother a brief farewell and hugged little Joe. As I was doing a potential errand of mercy for my new relations, she only commented six times on why Bertram could go without me.

'Richenda has never listened to me, ma'am,' said Bertram. 'Not even when we were kids. She was more likely to lock me in a cupboard and forget about me.' He said it in such a forlorn way that my mother made him drink a cup of tea as she lectured him on how a man needs to be strong with his female relations. I hugged little Joe, who was bright-eyed with curiosity, and I promised to be bring him back sweets or cake.

'Because you know Aunt Richenda will have loads,' he said.

'She will actually be your sister-in-law,' I said.

'But she's so old!' said Joe. I made him promise never to repeat this and went out the car where I found Fitzroy relaxing in the driver's seat with his eyes closed. I got in beside him. He opened one eye. 'Your mother or Hans? Holding us up.'

'Mother.'

'Good,' said the spy, closing his eye again. 'I won that bet with myself.'

'I'm not going to like your world much, am I?'

Fitzroy didn't open his eyes. 'If it was a likeable place we wouldn't be needed.' He paused for a moment. 'I did try to get you to think seriously about saying yes, despite your situation.'

'You did all that was fair,' I said.

He did open his eyes at that. 'Well, that's a first,' he said.

'What is?' said Bertram hurling his case into the back. 'Never mind. Drive, man, drive. Before Philomena catches me again.'

The journey to Stapleford Hall was long, but uneventful. We did not stop to eat – although we did have to stop for calls of nature, something Bertram found most embarrassing. I merely found it a relief. The countryside provided ample coverage for discretion. Of course, Bertram's situation was not helped by accidentally coming into contact with a patch of nettles. I asked no questions and I knew Fitzroy was on his best behaviour as he merely pointed out where there were dock leaves. When Bertram had retreated once more into the greenery to tend to his injured pride Fitzroy said, 'I do like him, but it surprises me he wants to live in the Fens. He does not appear a fan of nature.'

'Is the plan to get Richenda to leave while we search the Hall? I presume she and Glanville must have travelled up with the children.'

Fitzroy nodded. 'Plus, she should have Stone. Bertram can appeal to his sense of honour to return to his master. Is Merry with them as well?'

'I don't know.'

Bertram appeared from behind a tree and climbed back into the car. 'Neither of you say a word.'

'Who else went with Richenda?' I said. 'Did Merry go?'

'Yes, I think so. Along with Lucinda of course.'

Fitzroy and I turned around as one to stare at him. 'Lucinda?'

'You know, Richard's widow. Richenda could hardly walk into the Hall without her. Until the lawyers get their talons untangled it's going to be a bit of mess about who owns what. He told me once he was leaving me his mills. I do hope he was joking. I believe Lucinda's father built them up. Lot of family pride in it and all that. Would be just like Richard to leave them to me – cause bad blood and all that.'

'Of course, Hans must have sent for her after Richard's death. Poor girl. What a shock it must have been for her.'

'No,' said Bertram. 'She came down for the wedding.'

'Could this be the guest your mother mentioned when you first returned to the Mullers,' said Fitzroy in a tone that could not be said to be friendly.

'I did not get a chance to ask,' I said. 'She had declined coming to the wedding. I am sure my mother said so. She was not on any of the seating arrangements.'

'Apparently she decided she needed to be with Richard because of her fragile state.'

Fitzroy and I looked at Bertram blankly.

'You know. Interesting condition and all that.'

'Pregnant!' I said, my voice rising in alarm. 'How pregnant?'

'How the hell should I know?' said Bertram, tugging at this collar. 'Not the kind of thing one generally discusses. Only knew 'cause Richard started boasting about it to all and sundry.'

'I presume she did not come to the church because she felt unwell,' said Fitzroy. 'Did you see her, Bertram? Did her figure seem enlarged?'

'Good God, man! She's my brother's wife! I've never looked at her figure.'

'Oh, Bertram, you know that's not true. When we first met her at the castle you were quite taken with her,' I said.

Bertram began to bluster. Fitzroy interrupted. 'Enough of the marital disputes.' He turned to me. 'Are we considering her as a threat or a possible victim?'

'Either! Both!' I said. 'She may want to inherit Stapleford Hall now the Castle is partly burnt out. But there is nothing to suggest that she would do Richenda or her children any harm.'

'If only we knew whose idea it was to go to the Hall,' said Fitzroy.

Bertram shrugged and folded his arms, making a little snort.

I ignored these signs of sulking. 'At least we know she wasn't in the church.'

'Hmm,' Fitzroy. 'I don't like any of this. It feels all wrong.' He turned in his seat to face me and said quietly. 'I am aware this is your family, but our priority is to find the key to decode Richard's book. Anything else the regular police can deal with. The telegram I received...'

Bertram interrupted him. 'Would you mind very much not whispering in my fiancée's ear in front of me. It's bad enough you keep abducting her but making up to her in my presence is too much.'

Fitzroy swore violently. Bertram blushed, but by now I was used to the spy's way of letting off steam and barely noticed. 'Bertram,' I said. 'It's not like that...'

'Shut up, the pair of you,' growled Fitzroy. He turned on the engine and accelerated away so fast the tyres screeched.

I have no idea how long it took us to reach Stapleford Hall. I was far too busy praying for our survival. Fitzroy drove in a manner that can only be described as reckless precision. He avoided crashing by a hair's breadth on more occasions than I care to remember. He could only brake, turn, or swerve minimally. He appeared determined not only to minimise the length of the journey, but to keep the engine note so loud conversation was impossible. Despite this, I heard more than one yelp from Bertram in the back as he was battered about from one side to the other. Once I risked checking he had not been ejected by the sudden swerve, but the effort of turning my neck at this speed made it ache in an alarming way. In my mind's eye I suddenly had a crystal-clear memory of reading an article in a newspaper that opined that excess speed in a car would liquidise one's insides. At this point I closed my eyes and consigned myself to my fate. Even if I wanted to attempt it, I could never have wrestled the wheel from Fitzroy's grasp, and if I had, I suspected ending up in a ditch might be a preferable fate to facing his wrath. I only wished he had been able to tell me what was in the telegram. As I had told Bertram, we had been ricocheting back and forth between events, but my suspicion was growing that somehow everything tied together. If I survived the journey maybe I would find out.

A terrifying time later we drove through the gates of Stapleford Hall. Fitzroy at least slowed somewhat for our progression up the drive. I was grateful for this as the hall still had a free roaming flock of sheep. I might have explained this, but I had not yet gathered myself enough to speak. The spy on the other hand had a calm, almost beatific expression on his face. 'Ah,' he said, smiling at me, 'that blew the cobwebs away.' I managed to nod. Bertram made a strange noise from the back halfway between a groan and a growl.

I half staggered, half threw myself out of my seat before Bertram could help me down. I wanted some time to reacquire the ability to walk as much as I desired to feel good, solid, unmoving earth beneath my feet. Bertram similarity lurched out of the car and wobbled across to me. Fitzroy sprang out of the driving seat and near skipped up to the ring the doorbell. 'Does that fellow ever get on your nerves?' said Bertram.

'All the time,' I said quietly. Bertram grinned at me. His grin faded as he looked past me at the open door.

'Hello, Stone,' said Fitzroy. 'How's the new job? I fear Mr Muller is quite gone to pieces without you.' He said this is a nonchalant tone that clearly indicated he didn't care a jot for Hans' wellbeing. But it was enough of an opener to floor Stone for enough of a moment to let the spy breeze through the door and into the hall without explaining who he was or why he was here. I took Bertram's arm and urged him forward.

'Good afternoon, Stone,' I said. 'Our luggage is in the boot. If you could see to three rooms being made up? We will be staying at least the night. How are Mrs Stapleford and Mrs Muller? I believe Mrs Stapleford is a little overwhelmed by her condition. Might I hope she is doing a little better now?'

Even this oblique reference to pregnancy caused Stone's face to solidify more than usual into his signature non-expression. 'Good afternoon miss, sir. Mrs Muller is out riding. Mrs Stapleford is resting. Do you wish me to send a maid to awaken her?'

'Of course not,' I said. 'But I would very much like to come in. The ride across was cold. Do you think Mrs Deighton could summon up some tea and scones for the weary travellers?'

'That sounds excellent,' said Bertram, adding his force to allow Stone to step aside and let us in. I would have thought once one of us had got in he would have given way. I could no longer even see Fitzroy past Stone. He had obviously disappeared into the bowels of the house.

Stone did not yet give way. 'The other man?'

'The Inspector,' said Bertram. 'He's the man who helped

find Richenda's children that time they were kidnapped. Glanville knows him. I'm sure she'll give him a reference if ours isn't considered good enough.'

At this Stone did step aside. 'Not at all, sir, but this is not the first time the gentleman has got past me into an abode without giving his name or reason for entry. It is, I am not ashamed to say, a unique occurrence. I can only suppose the police are used to being given a free licence to enter.' Bertram's eyes widened. If I had not been so cold, I would have stayed to continue the conversation. For Stone to enunciate so many words in a single utterance was literally unheard of. I walked past him, calling over my shoulder, 'We will take tea in the blue salon.' I didn't wait to get a response. I wanted to know what Fitzroy was up to.

I found him, as I had expected, in what had always been the Stapleford master's office. Richard's father had used it when I had first arrived there, and later Richard when his father was mysteriously killed by a wandering tramp.[22] What did surprise me was that he had swung a picture aside and behind it had found and opened a safe. He appeared to be rifling through the contents.

'Hello, Alice,' he said without turning around. 'Nothing interesting in here. Just money, deeds and a copy of Richard's will.' He turned and tossed it to me. 'Check and see if Bertram was right about the mills, there's a good girl.'

'We're to have tea in the Blue Salon in a quarter of an hour or so,' I said, catching the will and drawing up a seat to the desk to examine it.'

'Good,' said Fitzroy. 'Do you think there will be

---

[22]One cannot help feeling that the authorities, by which I mean the police, have a singular lack of imagination when it comes to covering up murders by powerful people.

sandwiches as well? I didn't sleep much last night and, as you know, that always increases my appetite.'

'No idea. Bertram's right. The mills go to him. Everything else goes to Lucinda, unless she has a child, in which case it goes to the child in trust with her as trustee. Nothing to Richenda. There are also some small bequests of money to friends and staff that are to be taken out of the estate first. Goodness, he has even left me £100 for *being a good sport*.'

'Trying to wreck your reputation from beyond the grave?' said Fitzroy coming over to the desk. 'You really got under that man's skin, didn't you?'

'I tried to get him hanged for murder, but higher powers got him off. I don't suppose that was you, was it?'

Fitzroy held up his hands. 'Not personally, no. But he did have contacts, not only in parliament but on the more shadowy side of government. He might have had a black heart, but he was a devil for investments and his armaments company was becoming the most forward in the world.'

I frowned. 'I thought he was only an arms dealer?'

'At first,' said Fitzroy. 'Then he got a bit of a taste for the business, it seems. Started buying up and investing in a number of arenas. Then brought them all together under one roof as it were. He hid the business under a couple of shell companies – don't ask, it's very dull.'

'So, this business of finding Richard's killer to clear my name has all been a deception to… to what? Find weapons plans? Take over this company?'

Fitzroy leaned back against the desk and looked down at me. 'You know my department has been interested in Richard for a long time. Of course we want to know who killed him and why. We also want to get our hands on some documents he has.'

159

'So, it was not about helping me?'

'Let us say that I used the Richard situation to my advantage in getting you out of the mess you'd got yourself into. I believe I may even have said things like *invaluable assistance*, thorough knowledge of the grounds and participants, and even *vital to the operation.* Saying I liked you and didn't want to see you hanged wouldn't have cut any mustard with my superiors.'

'But you said that they – you – has been considering recruiting me...'

Fitzroy raised a hand to stop me. 'Let's get this over before Bertram comes in, shall we? Yes, my reports on our shared exploits and other independent reports...' I started to ask about these, but he frowned at me and held up his hand again. 'Other independent reports suggested you were a useful asset. I made a case that you were worth recruiting. It had won some favour and then you got yourself arrested on suspicion of murder. The department's reaction was to wash its hands of you. Your name and image was in various newspapers and people were talking about you. Very fast work, by the way; I suspect you have more enemies than you realise. We'll need to look into that. Anyway, as such my lords and masters considered you would be worthless as a spy, as your ability to go incognito had gone up in a puff of smoke the moment the first newspaper published your picture. As far as my department was concerned it was time to move on. However, there were still questions that needed to be answered about Richard Stapleford. I played that to my advantage.'

'You did recruit me? This isn't some kind of trick.'

'I can see how you might think that,' said Fitzroy calmly. 'It's one of the reasons I gave you the badge. Normally there's a bit of a probation period. But seeing as failing that usually ends in termination, I didn't see the harm.'

'I do not recall you mentioning that in your recruitment speech.'

'I didn't,' said Fitzroy. 'I find it puts people off. Besides, I was determined you – and I – would succeed and there would be no issue over your acceptance.' He tilted his head on one side. 'And you know I generally succeed when I set my mind to things. I had no intention of allowing you to come to harm at the department's hands, or anyone else's.'

I lent my elbows on the table and massaged my temples with my fingers. 'I am so confused. You said yourself that I am too well-known to be of any use.'

'You are marrying a man who lives in the Fens and as such will not be part of the London set. We might have to change your appearance for the next mission or so, but that's easy enough. Your mother, who might have made herself a particular nuisance, has retreated into the world of the church to enjoy her reign as a Bishop's wife. I have no doubt she will cause a great deal of trouble there, but it will not reach the ears of the general populace. You will cut and dye your hair for a while. I will continue your training and by the time you re-emerge from the Fens into the real world, you will be a very different person in both looks and demeanour.'

'You have it all worked out, don't you?' I said, still rubbing at my increasingly sore head.

'I have a plan,' said Fitzroy. 'It does require two things. Your compliance and our ability to decode Richard's book.'

'Did you know about the book? I mean before I found it?'

'I knew he must have stored certain pertinent information somewhere, but not where or how exactly.'

'What is it that is so important? Will it reveal his killer?'

'To be honest, Alice, the department couldn't care less who killed him. That's for the regular police. I only want to uncover it for you.'

I wiped my hands down my face and looked up at him. 'Are you at odds with your – our – department?'

Fitzroy shrugged. 'You could say I'm a bit out on a limb, but as long as we get what is needed everything will be fine. I've gone further off track before and come back in alright.'

'Thank you,' I said. 'But something's changed. Is it the telegram?'

'Yes, but I can't tell you about that yet. Where's your husband to be?'

'I would guess in the blue salon awaiting his scones. Both Richenda and Lucinda are unable to greet us. One out on a horse, the other laid up with morning sickness or some such thing. I don't know how pregnant she is?'

'Good point,' said Fitzroy. 'You'd better be the one to ask. Unless you think Bertram would like to do it?'

I refolded the will and tied it up. Thank goodness Richard hadn't used a seal. I handed it back to Fitzroy who closed the safe and swung the picture back into place.

'How many pages of numbers were in the book?' I asked. 'Where they all in the same hand?'

Fitzroy whipped round so sharply it was almost a pirouette. 'What are you thinking?'

'That the son carried on from where the father left off. Do you think that before their relationship went sour, Stapleford senior might have been training Richard to succeed him? We both agree he was a remarkably cunning man, but not exactly clever. If this code is as -'

'What would that mean?' interrupted the spy.

'Richard obviously knew the key by heart, yes?'

'I would imagine so,' said Fitzroy.

'If his father did too, why would anyone keep a copy of the key?'

'You are giving me grey hairs, Alice. Is there a point here apart from our imminent downfall?'

'We were almost certain Mrs Wilson had kept an incriminating diary on the family – one of the reasons she was kept on, despite her drinking. What if she recorded the key in there?'

'Would she have reason to know it?'

'As you know, it's almost certain she was Richard's father's lover.'

'The illegitimate girl in the asylum again.'

'Yes, Bertram and I hunted for the diary, but we never found it.'

'But you had neither unfettered access to the house nor someone of my calibre to aid you. Let's find Bertram and the scones and get on with this. We'll cover more ground with three.'

Chapter Seventeen

We found Bertram wrapping himself around a scone. 'You've eaten five!' I said.

Bertram did a bit of choking and then said, 'How did you know?'

'The gaps in the pattern on the stand,' I said, sitting down and pouring out tea.

'No sandwiches,' said Fitzroy sadly. I passed him a cup of tea. 'Explain to Bertram what we are looking for,' I said, pouring my own tea. Fitzroy looked pointedly at the scones. I passed him a plate with three on it. He held it out for another. I added it. 'Now, tell him.'

'Mrs Wilson's diary probably contains a key to a secret cipher that, if we decode it, will make my department very happy and then they won't disavow me for helping Euphemia out,' said the spy succinctly and bit into a scone. He then slurped some tea before he had even finished chewing.

'What?' said Bertram.

'You remember we looked for it when we were helping…' I broke off. I wasn't sure how Bertram would take hearing the name of the female journalist he'd fallen in love with and who had been subsequently murdered by one of Richard's cronies.'

Bertram set down his plate. A sign he was taking the matter very seriously. 'I remember. We never found it.'

'Fitzroy reckons it's worth us looking for it again. Especially now there's no one around to stop us.'

'Although either, or even both, women could appear at

any moment,' said the spy.

'We'd better eat up then,' said Bertram and crammed the majority of yet another scone into his mouth. Fitzroy finished his tea while chewing. Being the only one with any manners, by the time the others were ready to start the search I had barely finished my tea and had not even touched a scone. When neither of them was looking I put one in each of my skirt pockets for later. I rather suspected if either woman came upon us, uninvited and ransacking the house, we would be thrown out on our ears and without supper.

'I wonder where the children are?' said Bertram in a mildly worried voice.

'For the children of one family to be kidnapped twice within one year would be a sign of significant negligence,' said Fitzroy. 'Where shall we start?'

'The room Mrs Wilson used to occupy would be one space, but I would imagine it was thoroughly cleared out for subsequent occupants.'

'It is also a somewhat obvious if she wished to hide the material from the Staplefords.'

'She loved a drink,' said Bertram. 'What about somewhere in the wine cellar? Inside an empty bottle or some such thing.'

'Possible,' said Fitzroy. 'She could have changed her hiding place, but each time she did so she would have risked discovery. Plus, the fact that by the end she was a dipsomaniac, by your account, seems to make it unlikely she would have got up the willpower to do so.'

'So, where it is hidden is somewhere people would either not touch or where anyone, family or servants, was unlikely to go,' I said.

Fitzroy nodded. 'Exactly.'

'The gardener kept a poison cupboard, for rats and other

165

vermin.'

'Mrs Deighton knew her the longest,' I said. 'Perhaps talking to her might yield a clue.'

'Capital,' said Bertram, 'you do that and Fitzy here and I will go treasure hunting.'

'Fitzy,' said the spy, in a low growling voice.

'Won't do,' I said. 'Mrs Wilson had been on staff a long time before I arrived. Bertram, you can talk of time far before I came on the scene. Besides, she doubtless has more cake in the kitchen.'

Bertram's face lit up. 'She might even do me one of her enormous sandwiches like she used to when I was a child. That would take us right back to the old days.' He stood up. 'Things I have to eat for my country.'

The spy watched him go with narrowed eyes. 'Alice, I cannot help but feel Bertram's new hobby of bestowing nicknames may well shorten his natural existence considerably.'

I looked at him in mock surprise, raising my eyebrows and widening my eyes. 'Surely, you are thicker-skinned that that?'

'Sometimes,' said the spy, 'I wish you were a man.'

'So you could challenge me to a duel?'

'No. So I could punch you in the face.'

I touched his shoulder lightly as I got up. 'We'll find the book between us. Things will work out.'

'Hmm.'

While Bertram ate his way heroically through the house's supplies Fitzroy and I made a thorough search of the housekeeper's room. This was made considerably easier as the room had largely been cleared. The cast iron bed stood stripped in the middle of the room and an unopened trunk stood on it. The washstand bore the ewer and bowl. A rug lay on the floor. And a set of drawers that might once have been in the upper part of the house, but which was now worn and scruffy, proved to be empty.

'Looks like the last housekeeper has left. Unless they have given her another room,' said Fitzroy as he searched the tallboy for secret compartments.

I pushed the bed to one side so we could roll up the rug and check the floor and skirting boards. 'I doubt that,' I said. 'There is a small parlour next door that the housekeeper uses. I cannot think of where else they could put the two rooms near to each other and near to the kitchen and pantry.'

Fitzroy grunted an assent. We both got down on our knees and checked the floor thoroughly. Nothing.

The spy got up and dusted down his knees. 'These trousers will never be the same,' he said.

'Do we get a clothing allowance?' I said.

Fitzroy raised one eyebrow slightly and hooded his eyes. 'My dear, the department could never afford clothes of the quality I wear.'

I didn't rise to the bait. 'Where shall we go now?'

'As Bertram has not come trotting back with helpful information – I'm assuming he would be able to tear himself away momentarily from the tea cakes if he found out anything?'

'You have a large appetite yourself,' I said.

'I eat when I'm hungry, not simply whenever I see food.'

'Of course he would,' I said. 'He's not an idiot.'

'Shall we test your hypothesis and see if his cellar suggestion has merit?'

I nodded.

'To save time, might you show me which cellar is the wine one rather than leaving me to guess?'

I turned quickly so he could not see me blush and led him

down and through the servants' passages I doubted Bertram even knew existed.

The cellar was a large vaulted affair with slotted shelves for containing bottles on three sides. The house had been built by Richard's father and had no real age. However, the design of the wine cellar conjured up images of the centuries-old cellars that one might find underneath a castle. I had lit a lantern from the servants' passageway and found another by the door. I lit this one and passed it to Fitzroy even though he had not asked for his own light. He seemed quite comfortable in the dark.

The room had been left undusted – either to increase the aged resemblance or because no one came down here to check. I had nearly stepped through the doorway before I felt my nose begin to itch and my throat begin to burn. I swung my lantern in a high arc to get sight of the room. The bottles were arranged with their necks pointed outwards. One of the previous butlers had tied a tag on each end.

Fitzroy edged past me gently and went over to read one at random. 'This is an excellent idea. Avoids the possibility of disturbing the sediment.' He glanced over at me standing in the doorway. 'One does not have to remove the bottle to see what it is.'

'Unless one says vintage stolen diary by the house of Wilson, this is unlikely to be the place.'

'Very good, Alice. That's almost funny. But I note that these racks do not go to the edge of the walls. Have a look down the sides, will you? You're not scared of spiders, I take it?'

I did not bother responding.[23] One side of the rack stood

---

[23]Having long hair and living in country houses means far too often for my liking one gets a spider in one's hair. Especially if one is

two feet away from solid wall. I supposed I could slip down there sideways if I had to – and Mrs Wilson had been remarkably thin when I had known her. I checked the other side and found a wider passage. 'This goes somewhere,' I called.

'How enlightening,' said Fitzroy, who remained busy among the bottles.

I walked down this second passage, my skirt scattering dust kittens as I went. Clearly no one had been this way for a while. At the end the row of bottles widened out to my right into another smaller vaulted chamber. In the middle of it stood an odd thing. Consisting of a large wooden drum it had a lid that would be screwed down via a central pole. Closer inspection showed me that there were several spigots, four in all. 'I've found some kind of press,' I shouted.

Fitzroy didn't answer, but I heard his footsteps. Moments later he joined me. With the combined light of the two lanterns I could clearly see a carving of grapes on the side of the drum. 'A wine press,' I said. 'To what purpose?'

Fitzroy raised both eyebrows at me.

'I know what it is *for*,' I said. 'But as far as I know, the Staplefords never attempted to make wine. This is hardly the climate for it.'

'An impulse purchase, and talking point when one's showing off the cellar? Something to say to young ladies? Do you want to come down to the cellar and see my wine press? You said Richard's father was a bit of a cad.'

'Still seems an odd thing to do,' I said.

Fitzroy set down his lantern. He climbed up onto an jutting out stone I had not noticed and began to unwind the

working as a servant. Although not an experience I ever grew to relish, I could tolerate it until I managed to shake it out. Never try and brush one out. The result is exceedingly unpleasant.

lid. 'Perhaps we will find something interesting inside.'

'The remains of a previous enemy of the family?' I said.

'Fortunately, I believe Richenda to be too large to fit in here, but you could fit someone of medium height and build in it, certainly. I doubt anyone would find them – even a police search would likely miss this addition to the main cellar. Come over here and bring your light. It's a deep vat.'

I cannot say I was thrilled with this idea. I already had numerous unpleasant ideas rushing through my imagination. I decided not to voice any of them in case Fitzroy continued to evaluate my fear aloud. It took quite some effort to unwind the central pole to raise the lid. Fitzroy stopped to remove his jacket. He folded it carefully and then realising there was nowhere to put it, dropped it on the floor with a sigh. Some time later, during which he had uttered many grunts and a number of foul swear words, the lid was high enough for us to see inside.

The spy took a handkerchief from his pocket. He wiped his forehead and then attempted to get some of the grime off his hands. 'Your turn, Alice,' he said. 'You lean in and have a look. I'll hold onto your ankles.'

I must have registered alarm on my face, because he gave a crack of laughter. 'It's only as deep as the outside. Bring that light over.'

We held our lights up and peered in. The inside of the wooden drum was unstained. The press had never been used. In the bottom there were a number of squashed spiders lying with their legs akimbo among a thick layer of dust.

'Damn,' said Fitzroy. 'I got excited when I found it to be so tightly screwed down, but then I wonder if a woman could have tightened it so hard?'

'Wood shrinks and expands,' I said. 'This cellar is on the damp side. It could be that a natural expansion of the wood made the screwing mechanism harder to dislodge.'

Fitzroy nodded. 'I was thinking the same. Pity though.'

He stepped back and regarded the press. Then he went forward again. He repeated this exercise several times. Finally, he said, 'I was wrong. It isn't as deep as it looks. I doubt it... but to be on the ... can you find me a small broom, Alice? And quickly. Our time must surely be running out.'

I darted back into the passage and found that the small sweeping brooms and pans were still stored in at frequent niches. I lifted one and brought it back. I offered it to Fitzroy.

'Oh, I'm sure you know how to sweep better than me. You've been a professional and all that.'

I refrained from arguing. He had, after all, not asked me to help unscrew the lid. I leant in and swept up the spiders and dust. It took several passes and was made slower by my increasingly frequent need to hold my head aside and sneeze. Fitzroy failed to notice my distress. He picked up his jacket and gave it a good shaking to free it of dust. The atmosphere was so thick with it I could feel my eyes beginning to brim. Finally, I finished. My eyesight was bleary, and I kept coughing.

'Go back into the passage,' said Fitzroy taking the broom from me. 'You've done enough.'

I gladly left the room and made my way a short distance along the servants' passage, so that I was still in sight of the cellar doorway, but back in an area that had been recently swept. I brushed my eyes with the back of my hands, but they continued to flow with itchy tears. At least I had stopped sneezing, although my breath did not sound quite right, and I felt an odd pressure in my chest. I heard Fitzroy's

171

steps approaching.[24] At the same moment I felt a tickling at the back of my neck. As I had rested against the wall it sadly could not be my fiancé playfully sneaking up on me.

'Gods, Alice, you look awful. I'd lend you my handkerchief, but it's covered in dust.'

'I will be fine in a moment. Do you think you could take the spider off the back of my neck please, before it decides to go down inside my collar?'

'Turn around,' said the spy in an amused voice. 'Heavens, it's a whopper.'

'It would be,' I said.

'I'm not joking,' said Fitzroy. 'Hold this. I may need two hands to retrieve this fellow.'

He put a small book into my hands.

'You found it!'

'Hmm, yes, the press had a false bottom. That was inside along with some dried flowers and what looked like it might have been a pair of baby shoes once. Don't move. Got it! Do you want to see him, or shall I put him back in the cellar?'

'I can hardly see a thing,' I said. 'My eyes are streaming. Just take it away please.'

I heard him retreat. I ran my fingers over the book. It was of average width and height, but surprisingly deep. I could feel a thin ribbon that functioned as a marker. This was no cheap notebook. Fitzroy returned. 'Hang on to my arm. Let's get you to somewhere you can wash your face and splash your eyes. You're going all red and puffy. It is not a good look on you. We should rectify this before Bertram sees you and runs off in alarm.'

'You are sounding very happy. You are sure this is the diary?'

---

[24] I could recognise his gait by now.

'Positive,' said Fitzroy. 'I had a quick look and I think I even spotted the key. We shall both be in excellent standing with the department.' He gave me a quick grin, but I spotted the relief in his eyes.

Chapter Eighteen

Fitzroy guided me to a chamber where I could rinse my eyes. I had to describe the way, so it became like a game of blind man's buff. The spy's good mood continued. 'I flicked through it and I can tell you there is a lot of stuff in here that will be of interest.'

'How so?' I remained distracted by my itchy eyes.

'I expect it to prove that the Staplefords have been involved in illegal arms sales for generations. I acquit the original Stapleford of treason. He was a businessman, but the late Richard took things one step further. He identified ways of selling both to Britain and, covertly, to Germany.'

'We are not yet at war. How is that treasonous?'

'I suspect Richard listed his contacts in his book in code. If they are who they are I think they are it changes matters entirely.'

'How will this affect Bertram?' I said, my eyes filling with real tears. 'He will be disgraced.'

'Don't worry, Alice. I'm happy to say the information I believe I am about to uncover is highly sensitive. It will never be released into the public domain.'

'Thank God.'

I heard Fitzroy open a door. He guided my hands to the sink. 'Can I leave you here? I am eager to prove I am correct.'

'I can manage.'

'Find me in Richard's office.'

It took me some time to clear my eyes. In reality it must have been only minutes, but I worried my vision would never clear. I wanted Bertram to come and find me. It annoyed me, quite unfairly, that he sat comfortably in kitchen scoffing cake while I suffered. When I could finally see my face in the small mirror, I had a shock. I spent several more minutes making my hair look less like a dirty mop and calming the inflammation around my eyes. By the time I went to find Fitzroy I must have taken almost half an hour.

The spy looked up at my entrance. He grinned more widely at me than I had ever seen him do. 'You look positively gleeful,' I said.

'You look better too,' he said. 'Come here, Alice. I've barely started and look what I've found.'

I walked behind the desk to look over his shoulder. In front of him were scattered various pieces of paper with grids and letters. To one side lay Mrs Wilson's diary. Opened at one page he had circled three words. Richard's notebook lay above the sheet he had been working on. A lot of it appeared to be nonsense. Fitzroy drew a line under one group of letters.

'Otto von Wolff,' I said.

'Proves everything,' said Fitzroy. 'We abducted him because we thought he was an unwilling agent of the Kaiser. The department is going to give him another opportunity.'

'All the people Richard was working with were spies?'

'I wish,' said Fitzroy. 'That would be wonderful. No, I expect that they are either what we would term assets – no spy training – or specialists in scientific or other areas who have been persuaded to sell Britain's secrets to other countries.'

'Traitors?'

'Indeed.'

I shook my head. 'Are you thinking Richard was in it for the money or the power?'

'From what you've told me, he did seem to love having a sense of being in control.' He winked at me. 'Can't understand that myself.'

'I had better go and find Richenda,' I said. 'And no, I won't breathe a word of this.' I began to walk away, but my brain buzzed with thoughts. I stopped and turned.

'Does that mean one of your – I mean our lot – killed him?'

'Leaving you to take the fall in some obscure plot to recruit you? Possibly planned by me?'

I felt my blood pound in my ears. Every muscle I could feel tensed. Fitzroy tilted his head on one side, studying me. Then he got up and came around the desk. He put his hands on my shoulders.

'Alice, I don't know what to tell you. In a perfect world, perhaps the pieces would fit together that nicely, but this is not a perfect world. Also, my dear, I hate to tell you this, but in the scheme of things you are not that important.' He leaned in to whisper in my ear. 'In fact, I'm only very slightly more important than you to the department. It's the whole not the individual that matters.' He leaned back to face me. 'No conspiracy to enlist you, Alice. And despite your unfortunate experiences with me, and with Cole, the department and its agents very rarely kill. It's messy and leads to difficult questions being asked. Generally speaking, it's much easier to discredit or shame someone rather than kill them. Of course, if you believe you've come across a career killer, you need to arrange for the usual authorities to lock them up.' He released me. 'There ends today's lecture. Go and do your family duty. Find Bertram first will you, and send him to me? If you don't stop him eating cake, he won't be able to get out of the kitchen.'

I nodded, bemused by his manner. Sometimes I could see

Fitzroy clearly, other times he was as shrouded and as enigmatic as he appeared to others. As I walked away, I could already hear his pencil frantically scribbling across the paper.

I found Bertram still in the kitchen as expected. I surprised Mrs Deighton by giving her a hug. 'I'm afraid I am only here to convince Richenda to go back home,' I said.

'I thought that husband of hers would be worrying himself sick,' said Mrs Deighton, wiping her hands on her apron although they were perfectly clean. 'I told her she had to go back.' She smiled sadly. 'Not that it ain't been wonderful having all them little ones running around. And Merry back taking care of them. What with seeing you two as well, it's been quite like old times.' She sighed nostalgically.

I moved my gaze between Bertram and his crumb-laden plate. 'Err, um, sorry, Mrs D, but I'd better get back to finding that old book my chum wants a look at. Some mouldy old first edition of something.'

'It'll be up in the library. The new maids try to dust, but you can tell their hearts aren't in it. Not like when you were here, miss, you and Merry.'

We made our farewells several times and finally managed to escape. 'You are good at dusting?' said Bertram.

'Rubbish at it. It makes me sneeze. Merry and I used to swap. I'd do her share of the floors and she'd do the dusting, but more importantly, we found the diary. In the cellar.'

Bertram punched the air and barely managed to stifle his cry of glee. 'That's one in the eye for old Fizz-bang,' he said.

'He's decoding it now in the library. He wants your help.' I had thought the smile on my beloved's face couldn't have got any wider, but I was wrong.

'Wants my help, does he?' said Bertram and even his gait became more of a strut.

'I need to find Richenda and talk her back into going home.'

'Well, there's a lucky thing. Mrs D said she'd come back in just before I went down. She's likely even de-horsed by now. Never could stand the smell of a horsey woman.'

I left him to have his confidence knocked down by Fitzroy and went in search of Richenda. Where, I wondered, would Richenda go to relax in a home that was no longer her home.[25] There was a small boudoir on the first floor next to the library. It was an odd arrangement and I suspected it might have been designed to be an office, but being too close to the rest of the family had proved unendurable for both Richard and his father. Not being a servant, I walked into the room without knocking. Richenda lay on a day bed, her face ruddy from riding. It always surprised me that such a compulsive equestrian could fail to lose weight. Seeing her now after an absence of a few days I realised that yet again she had put on weight. There was no doubt in my mind that she was deeply unhappy. Without opening her eyes, she said, 'Oh, Mrs D, just put the sandwiches down on the table. I am sure I will able to manage a few.'

'It's me, Euphemia.'

Richenda shot up to a sitting position. 'Is Hans here?'

'No, he thought that it would only provoke an unpleasant scene if he chased you here himself. He asked me to speak with you. Bertram is downstairs.'

'You are charged with bringing me home? Or does he

---

[25] Arguably it was no one's home under their late father's will, but someone must be paying the servants, and Richard, being the one who most wanted to own Stapleford Hall, was liable to be the one doing that.

only want the children?'

'He hasn't charged me with anything except to deliver a message. He would like you to come back with us certainly, but neither Bertram nor I have any intention of dragging you back – and as for separating you from your children! Honestly, Richenda, I thought you knew me better than that.'

Instead of answering me Richenda burst into tears. I may have mentioned before that she is not a woman who can cry to advantage. I sat down next to her and put my arms around her shoulders. I managed to interpose a handkerchief between myself and her stickier aspects. I did nothing but utter calming words and stroke her hand until the sobs subsided. I knew any comments would be lost beneath her wailing.

I suppose I do not sound particularly sympathetic, but I could not help but feel that most of Richenda's woes were self-inflicted. To suddenly demand that Hans, who had always treated her with kindness, fall desperately in love with her was unreasonable. When she reduced her crying and said, 'He doesn't love me!' I am sorry to say I answered, 'That was never your agreement. He has always treated you well, has he not? He is the father of your twins and he has allowed you to shirk almost all the duties he might have expected you to do as his wife. You have never shown an interest in his people, his schemes for improvement of the estate, or even held a dinner party for him. You have had it easy, Richenda. He has spoiled you.'

Richenda pulled away from me as if I had slapped her. 'You did everything,' she countered.

'Only because you would not. I would have taught you if you had asked. I tried on more than one occasion, but you were uninterested. And yes, your husband is fond of me. Do you know why?' I continued without waiting for an answer.

'Because I have never taken his kindness in giving me a home for granted. I have done all within my power to be no burden and to do whatever task was required. If you feel that fondness has grown too far on his side, I cannot say that you have anyone to blame but yourself. You have shown him only how demanding you can be. You even told him that the engagement ring Bertram bought me was better than your own – and yours is a diamond big enough to take someone's eye out. Mine is merely a few small coloured stones.'

'But Bertram put such thought into yours,' burst in Richenda.

'And Hans didn't? The way you deported yourself in front of him made him think that you were only interested in the best, so of course he got you the biggest diamond he could afford. He has done all he can to make your marriage work and all you have done is take. The message he asked me to bring you was simply that he wants you back and will hire any servants you require to do any tasks you do not wish to do. You are spoiled. Utterly spoiled. The twins may be too young to miss their father – although I doubt it. You know how he dotes on them. But Amy must be confused and missing her papa. As usual you have thought only of yourself.' Even as I surprised myself as I spoke these words. I had intended to be kinder, but my discussions with Fitzroy about the impending war had brought home to me how much we all took for granted.

'My twin has been murdered,' said Richenda. 'My father was murdered. My mother too.'

'And you were close to none of them. You may have been under Richard's sway when you were younger but look me in the eye and tell me you ever loved him as a brother. I dare you.' Richenda turned her face away. 'The Stapleford family has been blessed with only two decent people in this generation: Bertram and you. Bertram did not like his family, nor how it made its money, but he was content to sit passively by until I came along. He broke with all elements except you. He has begun to forge his own way in the world, and it hasn't been easy for him. Hans has given you everything you have asked for and would doubtless continue to do so.'

'He needed my money.'

'That was the bargain you made. A marriage of convenience to get away from Richard. He could have lived quite separately from you, but he tried to forge a marriage.'

Richenda's shoulders drooped. 'I know. I am not good enough for him.'

'Then I suggest you try to be better,' I said curtly. 'You are an intelligent and capable woman and it is high time you stopped being so utterly self-obsessed.'

'Yes,' said Richenda in a very quiet voice. 'It is.'

I breathed a sigh of relief. At that moment the door opened, and Lucinda walked in. 'That was most interesting,' she said in a voice far different from the shy young bride we had met in the Highlands. 'I always thought you were a force to be reckoned with, Euphemia, but even I did not expect you to be so forthright. You are correct, of course. Richenda will always give way to a stronger personality than her own. It took me so little effort to convince her to leave her husband. It surprised even me.'

I looked up at the slender figure in a bright, royal blue day dress. Her blonde hair tumbled in free curls around her lovely face. Her eyes were as cold as stone. 'What happened to you?' I asked.

'You already know the answer,' said the bride. 'Richard.'

'You are not pregnant, are you?' I said. Slowly the pieces were falling into place, but I did not want to see the picture. I did not want to acknowledge how culpable I was.

'If I am not it is not for want of Richard trying. Did you know how good an actor he was?' she said to Richenda. 'He wooed me, Euphemia. I know, you always saw through him, but can you imagine how kind, how attentive he was to the daughter of a mill owner, who had thought she would never be accepted by society? He made the same bargain as your Hans. Marriage for my father's money. Only he also got beauty and innocence. Even my parents blessed our union. He convinced them too of how wonderful, how magnanimous he was. He promised he would keep the mill school and hospital running. Within a day of my father's death they were closed. Within a day.'

'I never met you before you married him,' said Richenda. She stood up and went to Lucinda before I could intervene. 'I would have warned you, given the opportunity.'

'You came to my wedding,' said Lucinda. 'You met me before I married him, and you uttered not one word of warning. Euphemia, as a virgin, I acquit of not knowing how he might treat me. But you were a married woman. A married woman, who knew how very much he needed an heir. I was nothing to him but a pretty vessel for his children. My thoughts, my feelings were of no account. Can you imagine how he used me?'

Richenda shook her head. 'I cannot.'

'You and Hans have children. Did he ever take you against your will?'

'No,' said Richenda, pale with shock. 'Of course not. He is a gentleman.'

'Your brother was not.'

'Dear God.' She turned back to me. 'Did you know?'

'I remember what your brother said at the expo,' I said. 'I feared he was not treating Lucinda well.'

182

'Did you tell her?' asked Lucinda.

'To what end? You were his legal wife... unless you asked for help there is no charge under the law that could be brought. No matter how wrong that may be.'

'I had made my bed and that entitled him to rape me in it over and over again?'

'No. But you killed him,' I said. 'You pretended to be unwell with morning sickness and crept out of your room and killed him before my marriage ceremony.'

'I did. I revenged myself on him, Richenda, and you all at the same time. I had thought only to ruin your wedding day. That you would be blamed for his murder was a sweet blessing.'

'You would have let her hang?' said Richenda. 'You are as much a monster as my brother was.'

'I was no monster till I wed him. He changed me. Either of you could have warned me. You could have saved me.'

'Would you have believed us? Besides, we – I - hoped he did care for you.' I asked. I rose slowly. I wanted to get Richenda away from Lucinda. Richard's widow was working herself more and more into a wrought state.

'It doesn't matter now,' she said. 'I am grateful to you, Euphemia, for coming here to finish your work on Richard's family. I will not go back to what I was. I will not live among the mills again.'

'Bertram is also here,' I said. I begin to get an inkling of her plan. 'He will know what you have done.'

'I think not. Your Bertram is a gallant gentleman. He will believe a beautiful young woman in tears.'

'He would never believe that. Besides, Richenda's children will inherit before you.'

'Richenda's children sleep sweetly under the influence of the gas lamp in their room. The maid left the window open and it extinguished the flame.'

Richenda gave a cry and went for the door. As quick as lightning Lucinda picked up a marble ornament from the nearest table and dashed it against Richenda's skull. My friend went down under the tremendous blow. She lay on the floor unmoving. A tiny ribbon of scarlet trickled from her hair across the floor. It grew wider as I watched.

But now Lucinda was coming for me. I could not help Richenda, even if she still lived, if I too became a victim. Unfortunately for me there was nothing nearby I could grab to defend myself. Lucinda lunged at me, the bloodied figure in her hand ready to strike down again. I ducked aside, as I had been taught, and grabbed Lucinda's arm as it passed me by. Using the momentum of the weight, I threw her into a sideboard. She went down with a crash. She was too light to break the furniture, but it fell backwards. The ornament smashed as she fell, but she was lithe, and she was back on her feet before I could close the distance. She now wielded a wickedly pointed shard of marble. She swung it again in a wide arc. This time attempting to cut. I dodged backwards. How could I get close without being skewered? Why hadn't Fitzroy taught me something more useful. I retreated slightly, but knew if I got back into the corner, she would get me. I felt something bang against my leg. I pulled a scone out of my pocket and threw it at her. 'Help,' I screamed at the top of my voice. 'Help!'

Lucinda faltered, momentarily surprised by choice of missile. Then she grinned. Though it was less a grin than an animalistic showing of teeth. Lips drawn back revealing gums. 'No one will come. They are too far away.'

'Lucinda, have sense. If you let me save the children, I will speak for you at the trial. I will say what a monster Richard was.'

'Too little, too late.'

I threw my last scone. Lucinda laughed. I readied myself for the makeshift weapon coming toward me. With an effort of will I did not know I had, I raised my forearm to catch it. Lucinda had not bargained on this drastic effort. The point sunk deep into the flesh of my arm. Almost blinded with the pain, I twisted my arm away, taking the weapon with it. The pain pulsed through me. Every nerve ending fired with pain. I thought I would split apart. As Lucinda approached, I managed to get my unharmed arm up and closed one hand around her throat. I squeezed her windpipe as tight as I could. She began to choke at once, flailing to get free. But I could feel my strength fading as blood flowed from my other arm. My vision was darkening. I thought of the children upstairs slipping silently into death. 'Help!' I screamed with my last breath. 'Help.'

My consciousness was fading fast. The door burst open and Bertram ran in. His eyes widened in horror, but he did not hesitate. He grabbed Lucinda and wrestled her off me. Behind him came Fitzroy. 'The children. Gas lamp. Upstairs.' I managed to say before I passed into unconsciousness.

When I came to, I was lying in Richenda's old bedroom. Fitzroy stood at the end of the bed frowning. Someone touched my face. I turned my head and looked into Bertram's loving face. 'The children.'

'All well,' said Bertram. 'Fitzroy got to the nursery in time. There will be bad headaches all round, but they, and Merry, will be fine.'

'Thank God,' I said and tried to sit up. I flopped back onto the pillows almost at once. Fitzroy started forward, then stilled. I saw the bandage on my arm.

185

'You lost a lot of blood,' said the spy. 'You will recover, but for now you are weak. I take it you used your arm to block the shard? Most brave, and most ill-advised.'

'I couldn't think what else to do,' I said. 'I kept calling for help.'

'We were too far away,' he said. 'But Bertram somehow knew. He bolted up the stairs. Saved your life.'

'Richenda?'

Bertram lowered his head.

'No,' I gasped.

'She is not dead,' said Fitzroy. 'But she has not recovered consciousness. A doctor was called. Stone will be driving them all back to the Muller estate. We have notified Hans of her condition. He was most distressed.'

'Glanville?'

'Trussed up in a cupboard, and most indignant,' said Fitzroy with a wry smile.

'What will happen to Lucinda?' I asked.

'Let her up, Bertram. She needs to see this.'

'No,' said Bertram. 'I most certainly will not.'

I leaned on his arm and pulled myself to a sitting position. 'Either you take me around my waist and show me, or he does,' I said to Bertram. Growling and muttering under his breath, Bertram helped me to my feet. He took me out to the gallery above the lobby. There below, the hideous multi-hued rug had that had been an eyesore at Stapleford Hall from the day I first arrived, was rolled up. Something was inside it. A body!

'How?' I asked Fitzroy.

'Bertram's wrestled her off you, but she fought like a wildcat and, being a gentleman, he did not use the force he could have. It was only when they reached the top of the stairs that he resisted harder, or he would have accompanied her down them.'

'She is dead,' I said flatly.

'Of course, I will turn myself over to the police,' said Bertram. 'I will plead accidental killing or some such thing.'

'You will do no such thing,' I said, looking at Fitzroy.

'I agree,' said the spy. 'This ties things up quite nicely.'

'Murderous bride attempts to finish off husband's family and accidentally falls to her death?' I suggested.

'You should write newspaper headlines,' said Fitzroy. 'Indeed, I think we should go with that.'

'But…' said Bertram.

'No,' said Fitzroy and I in unison.

'It's over,' I said to Bertram. 'Let it lie. I will be wholly exonerated, and you will be free of the bad blood within your family.'

'She's right,' said Fitzroy. 'I'll drive you both to the Bishop's Palace. I do not believe either of you should return to the Mullers for some time.'

'A quiet wedding,' said Bertram. 'Your step-father could marry us. If you agree?'

'But who would give me away?' I said.

Bertram sighed. 'I fear we only have one option.'

I looked over at Fitzroy. He grinned at me. 'I do look rather swish in a morning suit.'

Proudly published by Accent Press

www.accentpress.co.uk